Empty Nest Antics

By: KC Rice
Special appearance by Carl Rice

Book Cover: SCinders
Editor: Chriss Prokic
Publisher: A Brush and Pen
Frankfort, KY.
Once again, I want to thank my team for their time, dedication, and support. I honestly don't know where I would be without you. I love you!

Also by K.C. Rice

Blood Moon
Estranged

Deadly Passion
Deadly Passion
Anguish-Wil's Story

Tattered Series
Kaycee's Tattered Spirit
Reconciled
Revelation
The Tattered Series Box

Standalone
Under His Protection
Empty Nest Antics

Watch for more at www.pureromancekcrice.com.

I dedicate this book to my one and only, my husband, my best friend, my lover, my research partner, my heart, and my soul. Without him, this little piece of entertainment would never have been created. Thank you, Aldie, for loving me, especially during the times I was so unlovable-PMS, menopause, hot flashes, mood swings, the list goes on and on. You will forever be my heart, my soul, my rock – my everything!

I love you so much, and even more tomorrow.

Your Babygirl

By the age of fifty, most women can relate and feel this way.

Fuck You, Womanhood

Let me be the first to tell you, womanhood is not all people think it is.

Case in point, we spend most of our tween years looking forward to getting our boobs, wearing bras, and getting our period. Because let's face it, being a woman is the ultimate. Right?

Wrong!

Your boobs hurt … a lot.

Your face breaks out, and your stomach bloats.

Then the dam breaks, and Aunt Flo, the bitch of all bitches rips your insides out and destroys your vagina every twenty-eight days. Sometimes she really likes to fuck with you and arrives early, with no warning. Until the teacher calls on you to come to the board and answer a problem. You stand, and the whole classroom bursts into a fit of laughter and points at you. It's then Aunt Flo slams her fist into your gut and yells, "Surprise, I'm here!" And you realize everyone knew before you because there's a huge bloody spot on the back of your favorite stonewashed jeans.

The humiliation is unbearable, not to mention the stigma that comes with it and the inability to live it down. The haunting follows you through the rest of your school years … yes, you read that correctly, years!

And while we're on the subject of Aunt Flo and the many reasons we hate her, how about this one; I'm going to compare her to an irritating mother-in-law. Surprises you by arriving early, claiming she's just here for a couple of days, but she stays a whole fucking week! Bitching and complaining the whole damn time. And our husbands, let's not forget how compassionate they can be during our monthly walk through the garden of hell. It's like when our estrogen kicks in and their testosterone goes into overdrive. Every damn time the wind blows, they have a hard-on and want us to 'satisfy their need'. Doesn't matter if we're cramping, spotting, or the floodgates have opened, and every time we stand, it pours. No, no, no ... we have a mouth. And they want us to use it, with a promise, 'Of course, I'll make it up to you.'

Yeah, right.

You feel like shit, and you tell him, "You want to 'make it up to me'? How about you cook dinner, do the laundry, or here's a thought suck your own dick. I'm taking an extra strength whiskey and a shot of Tylenol and going to bed."

And yet, we endure this throughout our 'womanhood', with extraordinarily little bitching because, let's face it, we're women, and that's just part of it. The joyful part is the multiple orgasms we can have in one fuckfest, that is, if he knows what he's doing. Just sayin'.

We are given the joy of carrying the future of the world inside us for nine whole months, though sometimes it feels like years. Months of waking up puking our guts out and waiting to feel the first kick. Getting to see it on ultrasound and find out the sex. Heartburn, hot flashes, constipation, hemorrhoids! And lest we forget the stretchmarks that itch and burn, sleepless nights, evading our horny ass partner, who you swear if he says, "You look beautiful, you're sexy as hell pregnant," or "I love you just the way you are," one more fucking time you're cutting his dick off.

"I'm fat. I'm miserable, and I want my body back. I want to be able to take a shit without ripping my asshole."

Why can't men understand it's not all about them?

The time finally comes, and your water breaks. Oh, sweet joy, the baby is coming. Soon he will move out of my uterus, and my body will be mine. I'll be able to tie my shoes, shave my legs, sleep and poop! But it's not that simple. This little shit has taken on his daddy's demeanor, stubborn and refusing to evacuate. The cramps you struggled through during your period are a walk in the park compared to the pain you're enduring now. You beg for an epidural and sigh in pure bliss as you feel the medication flowing down your spine and through your veins. Ahhh, yes. I can do this.

The time comes to push, and even though you threaten to kill your partner if he looks down there while you're pushing a 10lb baby out your hoo-ha, you no longer care who sees you all spread eagle as long as they get this kid out. Suddenly you hear his cry, and all is well ... for the moment.

They place him on your chest, and he nuzzles your breast and flips the switch. The next day you wake up a dairy cow. Your milk has come in, and your sweet little man is too impatient to latch on. He's screaming like a banshee bringing every nurse on the floor rushing in to see if he's ok. Your boobs are engorged and have relocated to under your arms, they ache and thump with every beat of your heart, and all you want are your itty-bitty titties back.

Oh, the joys of motherhood tacked onto the joys of womanhood. Yes, this is the life. You get into a routine and realize every time the baby nurses; it burns calories. Your 'baby fat' begins to melt away, and you have your body back and your sex drive. Score!

You pump a bottle of milk and drop the baby off at your mom's for the evening. Rush home and tidy up your neglected *she* parts. Smiling ear to ear because you can finally see your garden and give her a good weeding. You can't wait for daddy to get home. He is going to be so surprised when he comes through that door. And he is!

The candles are lit, sultry music playing in the background, and you splayed out on the bed waiting for your man.

Everything is perfect, his eyes smolder, and his soldier is standing at attention. He can't get his clothes off fast enough. He cups your breasts, and his mouth waters as he sucks a nipple deep into his mouth. Your back arches and the electricity zings through to the apex of your thighs, yes! It's been so long, and you are willing to do anything he asks at this point. And just the thought makes your body sing. But he jerks away from you as though you had electrocuted him, spitting, cussing, and gagging.

What the fuck? All hell flew into you, you're hurt, angry, and desperate for release, and he's backing away from you, spitting with a look of disgust on his face.

He finally looks at you and sees the look on your face. His disgust changes to fear as he realizes he's fucked up. He immediately begins to apologize, something about a mouthful of milk, and it tastes nasty. How can the baby drink this shit? Yeah, he just keeps digging his hole deeper and deeper.

You quickly jump off the bed and head toward the bathroom slamming the door behind you as he yells, "Honey, I'm sorry. That milk is nasty ... have you tasted it?" Gag, "I wasn't expecting to get a mouthful. Look, I'm sorry. Let's start over. 'Mr. Happy' is sad, and he wants to make it up to you. Come out here and look."

Yeah, yeah ... once again, it's all about the man.

The years go on, and your family grows. You find yourselves hiding in closets and laundry rooms just for a quickie and grateful for each one because, without it, your sex life would be zilch.

The kids grow and finally graduate high school, head off to college, and move out. The house is finally yours. You're free. You can run around the house naked. Hell, clothing is optional, have all the sex you want, and damn if you aren't horny and feeling kinky as hell ninety-five percent of the time. You can be as loud as you want, no more biting a pillow. Scream, baby, scream!

But then something happens, you can't really explain. Your body begins to change. You skip a period here and there. And you notice a hair growing from your chin. What the hell?

Menopause!

A whole new level of excitement begins to grow within you. No more periods. No more cramps. You look forward to Aunt Flo's last visit before she retires, and finally, it comes. But she leaves behind a whole other sack of shit.

That one chin hair turns into a whole family, and then they have neighbors move in on the other side of your chin. Your stomach begins to expand, and you go from a size ten to eighteen in a year. No matter how much dieting and exercise you do, the heavy flabby fat refuses to let go. And then there are the hot flashes that make you feel like your body is melting from the inside out. You wake up in a pool of sweat every morning and try to reason with the man upstairs, "If I'm going to sweat like a pig, could you at least make it melt this fat off my gut?"

You step out of the shower, see your reflection in the mirror, and realize your mother is staring back at you. When the hell did this happen?

Sexy? No, I'm not sexy. I'm my mother made over.

Your partner starts with that old bullshit again ... you know the adulation he uses just to get into your pants. "You're beautiful ..." as he reaches around, grabbing your 'peter pouch', as he calls your flab. "I still find you sexy as hell, and you look great for a woman your age who's had three children and gone through menopause."

Your hand begins to itch, and the desire to bitch slap him consumes you. You have to make a fist and call on all your strength to hold back your mother from once again overtaking your body and following through.

Swallowing your pride, you're still horny as hell and want to try out some new things. Add some spice to your love life.

But then mother nature has different plans. You see, that crazy-ass bitch isn't satisfied with all the shit she has already put you through. No, she had one last good jab before calling it quits. It wasn't enough that she demolished your sexy girlish figure, erecting in its place a mausoleum. No, she had to close down the sex department and dry up the stream of desire. Replacing it with exhaustion, headaches, and a dry pit of despair. Your partner complains you aren't 'wet' enough, so you buy a lifetime supply of Astro Glide only to have him complain of the taste. Well, fuck me.

But, for those who were blessed and born a boy, well, you are a lucky little bastard.

No cramps, no periods, and you can scratch any itch you have anywhere, and no one would think ill of you. Find yourself in the middle of nowhere, with no bathroom in sight? No problem, just whip it out and let 'er go, no TP necessary. Masturbation is expected, not frowned upon. And orgasms, though you only have one per fuckfest ... at least men are guaranteed to have one. Women must focus hard, willing our bodies to accept the passion, pushing every sensation to the apex of our core, zeroing in on every nerve ending that dwells within the region, yet still, we are not guaranteed.

Men, wham bam ... push and thrust. Explosion!

They don't have to endure hormonal changes or sharing their bodies with another human. Stretchmarks, birthing pains, hemorrhoids, engorged breasts. All this and still keeping a home, working full time, cooking, cleaning. The list goes on and on. Women don't get time off, even when sick. But a man? A mere common cold will have him curled up in the blankets, summoning you for more medication, a drink, a cool rag, and sometimes even crying for their mommy.

Yes, indeed, it is safe to say men have life easy, and it sucks donkey dicks.

When they begin to age, their sex appeal grows alongside them. Women spend a fortune coloring their hair because gray on a woman is taboo. But men? They have transformed from a stud muffin into a sexy gray fox.

Their center grows wider, and they aren't fat ... no, they have the sexy 'dad bod'. And who in the hell decided bald men are sexy? Don't get me wrong; I'm just as turned on as the rest of the female population. A man's hair starts thinning, and he simply shaves it all off. *Voila!* Another sexy, hot as fuck look.

We, women, endure a lot in our lives, the good, the bad, and the ugly, and there is a lot of ugly. Fuck you, Eve!

We savor the miracle of birth, after the fact, of course, but still.

We and we alone control the 'goods'.

And though we grow old, and our bodies betray us, we find ourselves wishing for our youth to return or at least a glimpse of a memory of the way it once was. We will always have a partner in crime, an ace up our sleeve, and someone to have our backs. Mother nature, though you've fuck us over again and again throughout our lives, we know we can depend on your evil twin in the end.

Wait, the story is not over yet.

Remember the men? The lucky assholes who thought they ruled the world and were invincible. Who thought they were the best lovers and never had to deal with the shit we women do? Those very same men who 'aged gracefully with pizzazz and sex appeal'.

Yes, those men.

One day, they wake up and try to get their freak on only to find he no longer rises to the occasion. They whine and complain, "My winky's broke," and their world is crashing around them.

Yeah, well, now it's our turn to lie to them and say, "It's ok, I still find you sexy as hell, and you still have your magical tongue. That's all that matters."

Yep, Mother Nature's evil twin appears out of the blue. What's her name?

Karma.

How it all began

"Well?" My best friend, Beckee, asks while arching her brow at me suspiciously.

"Well, what?" I answer her, rolling my eyes and laying on my thick, southern twang, dismissing her accusatory look.

She laughs and swats my arm. "Lisa Gail, what are you and Alex going to do with all your time? I mean," she pauses for a moment, "I remember how lonely the house seemed when I first discovered the empty nest. I can't imagine your baby girl is all grown up and off to college." She sips the last of her cola through her straw, making the awful gurgling sound. I cringe and grit my teeth. That bitch knows how much I hate it when she does that.

Jerking the empty glass from her hands, "Give me that," I scold, slamming it on the table. "You know, Alex and I aren't your typical parents. Hell, he's already screwed two hooks beside the front door and hung robes on 'em."

"What! Why in the world did he do that for?" Reaching for her empty glass, giving me the evil eye as I jerk it from her reach and smirk.

"I was going to eat my ice, thank you very much. Now give me my glass, please."

Getting our waiter's attention, I ask for a refill handing him the empty glass. He nods and turns, walking away with it. I glance over the rim of my glass, sipping my sweet tea. "Mmmmm, if only I were twenty years younger," I mumble before sitting back in my seat.

Tearing my eyes off his sweet tight buns, I'm a bit taken back at the glare I'm receiving from my bestie. "What? Oh, like you didn't check out his ass when he first came over here. I saw you," I throw my napkin across the table, hitting her in the face. "Don't act all holier than

"

thou. I've known you too long; you're probably sitting over there in wet panties."

Beckee's eyes look over me, and her face turns crimson as her jaw hits the table. I already know why ... He's standing behind me. He'd heard my comment.

Shit.

Luckily for me, I'm quick on my feet. Smiling, I turn, giving him a playful wink. "Are you married?"

Beckee chokes on her Coke, drawing my attention back to her as she sprays me in the face with the sticky liquid. Her eyes are as big as silver dollars, and her drink drips from her nose.

"It's ok, Beck, I wasn't asking for me," I look back at the young man standing beside our table, "I'm happily married. I was asking for my daughter." I dismiss with a flick of my wrist before declaring proudly, "I've been with the same man for thirty-one years. Damn, I think I deserve a medal."

Matt, our poor unsuspecting waiter, looks back and forth between Beckee and me with a questioning look. "Is there anything else, ladies?" The look on his face tells us both he's afraid of what our answer may be.

"No, just the check, please," I reply as I watch him release the breath he had been holding. Turning on his heel, completely unaware two middle-aged ladies were watching, no gawking, at his sweet ass and the way those tight jeans fit as he walked away.

"Damn!" We both hissed.

I turn and look over my glasses, throwing her the look I've mastered over the years of being a parent. You know the one. Chin down, and lips tightened while I look over my glasses instead of through them in disbelief.

"What?" Beck asks defensively, "Ok. Ok." She holds up her hands in surrender. "He does have a very well-defined ass. That's all I'm sayin'."

I sign my credit card receipt, leaving a twenty for the tip, taking one last swallow from my tea, wishing I had gotten a glass to-go.

"Where to now?" I ask, placing my purse strap on my shoulder as we step out the door. The hot, muggy August weather, smacking us both in the face.

"Damn it," Beck sighs, lifting her long brown hair off her neck, "I wish it would rain and cool things off a bit."

Looking up to the cloudless sky, twisting my hair up and into a messy bun nodding in agreement. "Are you kidding? It's August in the South. The only thing you can expect while here is hot, sticky, sweltering temps. I swear I think it gets hotter and hotter each year."

Beckee rolls her eyes and clicks her tongue, "Bitch it ain't getting hotter; it's your damn hormones. That's spelled, W.H.O.R.E.M.O.A.N.S. by the way." She laughs and ducks just in time, my hand missing the back of the head as I try thumping her.

"Hey, you're older than me." I laugh, joining in her humor.

She links her arm through mine, "Damn, I've missed you so much. We need to do this more often. Next time, you come to visit me. It's cooler in the North."

"I know. Let's set a date soon. I'm sure my calendar will be filling up quickly now that Alex and I are free." I smile.

"Speaking of Alex, why in the hell did he put hooks up by the door again?"

I try to stifle a giggle, "You know, to hang our robes on." Shrugging, "Just in case."

Perplexed, she asks, "In case of what?"

"Someone stops by ..." I take a step, but she jerks my arm back.

"Wait, what are you ..."

I interrupt her, "Alex's declared clothing optional at our house. He walks around butt naked. I told him one day someone will come to the door, and he's going to give them one hell of a show. That's when he got the bright idea of putting our robes beside the door."

She takes a step back as her mouth drops, "Oh. My. God! Are you fucking serious?"

"Yep! He's even talked me into it a few times." Shrugging, "It's comfortable and, as a bonus, saves on laundry. I stopped participating because he would sneak up behind me, bend me over whatever I'm standing close to, and act like he's drilling me from behind."

Beckee bursts with laughter, "*Omg*! Your husband is a hot mess. So, why'd you stop? Back in the day, you would have jumped at the chance of being drilled from behind."

We both laugh out loud at her comment because we both know it's so true. Wiping the tears from my eyes, "Every time Alex did it, I would burst out laughing. He would say, 'Here, I am trying to get my groove on, and you're laughing at me'. After a few times, he just stopped. I seriously think I hurt his feelings. I didn't mean to; it was just the way he would do it. It was funny."

"You are so damn lucky. I wish I could have found a man like him; he's one in a million, Lisa."

Smiling, my heart swells at her comment because I know firsthand how true her statement is. I am the luckiest gal in the South. I also know I truly don't deserve him. What he sees in me? Hell, I have no idea, but I sure am glad he sees something. I owe him so much. I am a blessed woman.

My mind races as we continue our walk. The thoughts that had been consuming my brain as of late flashing past like a strobe light. Then I think, if I can't talk to my best friend about this, who can I talk to? Straightening my shoulders, I lick my lips and take a deep breath. Here goes.

"Beck ... I have a confession to make. Well, I don't know if it would be considered a confession or a declaration. Either way, I need your advice."

Beckee spots a bench under a shady tree and motions, "Sure. Of course. What's wrong?" The worry etched in her face, filling me with more emotions, causes my eyes to tear.

"I'm not sure where to start ..."

Taking my hand, Beck encourages me, "It's me, Lisa. I hope you know after everything we've been through that you can come to me with anything. I won't judge. What's wrong?"

Pulling my hand free of her clasp, I wipe my palms nervously on my shorts, take a deep breath and begin.

"My body hates me, plain and simple. I thought once I went through menopause and had no more surprise spotting or periods lasting weeks at a time, life would be much better. But instead, it hates me. I've begun to grow hair where no woman should have hair, well not like this anyway. Do you see this?" I point to my chin.

Taking my face in her hand, Beckee searches, "I don't see anything. What am I supposed to be looking for?"

"*This*! I can find the mother fucker without a mirror." I grasp the stiff hair that had taken up residence on my chin between my fingernails and pull on it. But to no avail, the damn thing doesn't budge.

"See! I'm growing a fucking goatee. And no matter what I do, the damn thing won't die. I have used everything on the market to get rid of this pain in the ass hair, even plucking it, but I swear it is rooted in my jawbone. It *will not* come out. And it's stiff, like a damn whisker. What the hell? And this morning? When I was sitting in my car minding my own business, I might add, putting on my lips, the sun shone in on my chin, just at the right angle. This fucking hair has either reproduced or is having a damn party on my chin."

Defeated, I drop my shoulders and sulk while my best friend looks at me like I've lost my mind. She opens her mouth to say something, but I cut her off before she can utter a word.

"I'm not done yet." I interrupt her, "Then there's the weight. I have gained thirty pounds in one year. I used to have a nice body. Well, I admit I only had boobs when I was pregnant or nursing, but I've always had a nice ass. Ask anyone. But now, it needs a backup alarm."

Jumping to my feet, I swing my ass over in front of her, "See! Look at this ass! It's huge!" I smack the cheeks of my ass with my hands. "Alex says he loves my ass. I told him it's a good thing because there's plenty of it." Plopping my fat ass back on the bench, I look over at my bestie, expecting to see sympathy. Instead, I'm floored. She's laughing her ass off. At my expense. *WTF*!

She quickly notices the frown on my face and clears her throat, trying to compose herself, "I'm sorry. It's not funny. Really, it's not, but the look on your face and your expressions ..."

"I'm serious, Beck. And let's not forget the worst part of it."

"Oh, you mean there's more?" The smirk on her face is still visible as she asks.

I cock my brow at her and give her 'the look'. She knows she's digging her grave deeper and deeper. Beck also knows my temper, and it's not good. My bestie straightens her spine and places her hand in her lap, like some prim and proper lady. Yeah, right.

"I'm sorry, Lisa, what's the worst part, babe?"

"Promise me you won't tell anyone. I mean it. I have a reputation to uphold, you know." She crosses her heart and pinky swears.

"My sex life is non-existent. I mean it, it's like blah. I think the biggest issue is my damn hormones. It's like the flames have been snuffed out, without any hopes of a spark to rekindle them. I think Alex and I need to find a way to add spice to our sex life. I think that's the key, like maybe we've become complacent. We need to stir the ashes and get our fire roaring again, but I don't know how. Help?"

Beckee sits back on the bench and thinks for a few moments, and I can tell when the lightbulb goes off in her head. Her eyes glisten, and a shit-eating grin forms slowly across her face. Turning, she looks me deadpan in the eyes.

"Two words. Fifty Shades."

I'm dumbfounded. Seriously, I just poured out my heart and soul, and she's talking about ... "What the hell is Fifty Shades?" I jump up and start pacing in front of her.

"What?" She acts shocked, "You've never heard of the book series? Oh my God, Lisa. It's the latest rave; it's been talked about all over the world. Some women have even sworn it's turned their marriage bed into an inferno. I have all three books. Here, I have them on my Kindle app and can loan them to you." She swipes her phone and opens her app. I watch as her fingers dance across the screen, still wondering what the hell this Fifty Shades is about.

"There ya go, babe, just sent you the first book. You have fourteen days to read it." The look on her face is like she's solved the world's biggest problem, she is strutting her stuff, and it's getting on my nerves. How can she know about this 'sex book' if that's truly what it is, before me? Oh yeah, it's because I don't read much. Perhaps I need to start?

She drops her phone back into her purse, satisfied with herself. "Read the damn book. You and Alex will thank me." She wiggles her eyebrows suggestively. "When you finish, let me know, and I'll send you book two. Oh, you might want to stock up on batteries too." She snickers as though she knows something I don't.

Again, I give her 'the look,' my stink eye, as we come to a stop beside her car.

"Seriously, Lisa. I have faith in you, use your creativity, draw out that inner slut, let her out to play. If anyone can do it, it's you." She pats my cheek, "I have to get my ass on the interstate and head up north. Love ya, babe."

"I love you too," I give her a tight squeeze. "Thank you, Beck, for everything."

She hugs me back before slipping into her car, "I'll call you when I get home. Read the book."

"Yes, ma'am."

I watch as my bestie backs out of the parking spot and drives away, more determined than ever to stoke the flames and send my sexy hubs into pure sexual bliss.

I pull into the drive and sit, staring at our empty house. The song on the radio ends, and Cher's *If I Could Turn Back Time* starts to play. I lay my head on the headrest and close my eyes, remembering the music video. Alex drooled every time it came on while I envied her. It was obvious she was comfortable in her skin and the sex appeal that poured off her as she sang and danced along the aircraft carrier, driving the men and women crazy for different reasons. I mean, good grief, she was, what, fifty years old when she did that video? God, I would give anything to have that body and the confidence.

The song ends, "Ok, Lisa. Get over your pity party. So, you're forty-five. There are a ton of men and women like you who are facing the same issues. It's all in how you decide to handle it. Do you stick your head in the sand and feel sorry for yourself, or use your head? Do some research, take that step of faith in yourself, and become who you want to be. It's only too late when you're dead and buried. So, stop wasting time! Get on with it girlio."

I raise my head off the headrest with a renewed determination, and my heart feels lighter. Happier with each beat, and I find myself feeling a bit giddy. Ok. Let's do this.

Turning the car off, I step out into the hot summer air and head inside to find and open the Kindle my hubs had gotten me for Valentine's Day.

My First Time

It took me a good half hour to figure out how the Kindle worked; I ended up calling my sister. After fussing at me for just getting around to opening it, she finally talked me through the programming steps. Damn, it would be so much easier the old fashion way, book in hand and dog ears to mark the pages. When I made that comment, I thought she was going to come through the phone and bitch slap me. How was I to know it's a big no-no in the book world?

"Bibliophiles would never be caught dead abusing their books with folded ends," she snapped at me.

I had no idea what the hell she was talking about, a biblio-what? Is that some new kind of religion, and the members think it's sacrilege to put dog ears in books?

I thanked her for helping me and hung up on her when she asked what book I would be reading. I mean, geez, after all the stress of programming my Kindle, I didn't have the energy nor desire to listen to her goading me about my choice of book. After all, I teased her about reading all those 'smut books' when she was a teen and young adult. And now, look at me! Talk about calling the kettle black. I'm getting ready to read a damn porno.

I swiped up the screen to unlock my Kindle and do a quick search, just to familiarize myself. Ok, who am I kidding? I was looking for the damn book. Where the hell did she say to look?

Swipe. Flip. Swipe.

Ahh ha, there you are!

My stomach began to flutter, like butterflies taking flight as I opened the book file. I was getting a little giddy, like a teenager sneaking a peek at her older brother's Hustler magazines. You remember the 'shit, what if I get caught?' feeling. I glanced over my shoulder to make sure no one was there and remembered Alex was at work, and I had the house all to myself. With no one to catch me reading porn, I gathered a fresh cup of coffee and settled down on my favorite corner of the sofa.

Anastacia Steele seemed a lot like me, timid and inexperienced. As I read further along, I soon convinced myself that the main character and I were kindred spirits. I could totally relate.

Christian Grey, damn. Before I knew it, I was sucked into a vacuum. The story took me into a world where I was Anna, and I wanted Mr. Grey to do all those naughty things to me. Shit, it got hot in here. My mouth was as dry as a popcorn fart, and my lower regions? The only way to describe them was on fire. It was at that moment I decided I needed to take notes.

As I jumped up to get a notebook and pen, my knees nearly buckle, fuck! I caught myself before I face-planted into the coffee table. The book had obviously affected me more than I realized.

Hot damn, Beckee, you were right.

I grabbed a notebook and pen from my desk and settled back down on the sofa. The young woman came to life inside me as I began reading again.

The book completely enthralled me, and the time of day was lost to me. The front door opened, and my very own Christian Grey walked through the door. He had his empty travel mug in hand and his baseball cap on backward. Damn, he was so fucking hot. My stomach flipped, my lady bits quivered, and I couldn't help but squeeze my thighs together to stifle my ache.

Alex noticed, his brow arching as he set the mug on the table beside the front door. His eyes locked on mine, making my stomach jerk and twist in response to the devilish look he gave me. He knew me so well.

I dropped the Kindle to the floor as he sauntered closer to me, his hand slowly dragging down his zipper. My eyes never left the bulge straining there. Wait! When the hell did he unfasten his belt? I yelped suddenly in surprise as his cock sprang free of its confinement, standing proud, and looked straight at me.

Frozen at first, unsure how to react, I sat before my husband dumbfounded until my imagination kicked in. Now I wasn't talking about just little giggly thoughts flowing through my mind. Hell no! It was full-on. Like the body snatchers or something, my body had a mind of its own, and it was downright scary at first. Then I saw the spark in Alex's eyes brighten into an inferno.

My hands began to wander of their own volition, Alex's eyes smolder while he watched me palm my breasts, squeezing them gently at first, but I soon turned up the heat. An instant zap of electricity flowed through my body, causing my girlie parts to clench.

My eyelids fluttered closed, and my mouth opened, a moan leaving it as I feel the sudden but delicious pain penetrate my nipples. My fingers continued their torture. A move I would later title the 'Triple Ts'. Tweak, Twist, and Tug.

I felt the moisture building between my thighs, the heat building, and just like that, one of my hands was swirling my clit. I was lost in the incredible pleasure my hands continue to exact upon my body. Lost in the excitement, in the fire burning deep inside my soul. Lost in the orgasm building higher and higher, like a pebble that's been tossed into a shallow pond, the ripples fan throughout. My body started to quiver, goosebumps spreading along my skin, my back arched, taking my breath as I came crashing down.

I was completely wrung out. Comatose.

Floating on a cloud of pure ecstasy, the heat that only seconds ago had my skin on fire now turned to ice, as the vent to the A/C above me blew across my fevered skin. The simmering sweat now turned to icicles and woke me from my erotic dream.

Caught Red Handed

I opened my eyes and felt the heat of my embarrassment while it slowly traveled up my neck and onto my face. Alex was home *and* standing in the room, watching me. OMG! Couch, please swallow me up.

Completely humiliated, I closed my eyes tight and willed myself to disappear. Never in my life had I ever masturbated in front of Alex. In fact, I've always denied it when he would tease and ask me if I thought of him when I did.

"*No*! I don't do that. It's gross. I've never masturbated. *Ever*!"

Busted!

To say I was utterly humiliated was the understatement of the century! The fire still smoldered in my belly, my lady bits tingled, and my fingers were wet. I quickly swung my legs off the couch and sprang to my feet. The moment they felt the carpet, I lunged forward and ran to the bathroom and slammed the door before locking it. Determined, my ass was staying there indefinitely.

Still feeling dumbfounded, I looked around my new living quarters. I can do this; I can sleep in the tub. Wait! Opening the door to the linen closet, I sigh in relief. Thank God I actually folded and put away the clean towels. I could use them to make a bed. Checking the closet, I was relieved to find a new pack of toilet paper and toothpaste; I was good to go. I flipped the lid to the toilet and took a seat, planning my new life. I had a bed, blankets, a pillow, so what if they were all towels and my very own toilet. Yep, I could eat, sleep, and shit without leaving the room, that was until the toothpaste and toilet paper ran out. Fuck!

"Sweetheart, come on, open the door." My husband insisted as he continued to knock. "It's no big deal. We all do it!"

Knock-knock-knock. "Come on; you can't stay in there forever. You'll eventually get hungry. What are you going to eat, the toothpaste?"

I was burning up, no longer embarrassed but madder than hell. I hated him! I hated him for coming home on time. I hated him for not knocking on the front door; I don't give a rat's ass that he lived here. The son of a bitch should have warned me he was home before barging in on me. And now the asshole was laughing!!

"Honey, come on, let me in." He giggled, "If you want, I'll rub one out while you watch, and then we'll be even." His giggles had turned into roaring laughter.

My head started to hammer; I was gritting my teeth so hard, trying to keep my mother from coming out in me. I seriously didn't know how much longer I could hold her off.

"Come on, baby, seriously. Open the door. Let me in." My husband pleaded. I could tell by his muffled voice he had his head against the door. "Sweetheart, we've been together over half of our lives. I've seen you at your best and your worst. I've seen you stretched wide open, giving birth to both our kids. I've held your head while you've puked and wiped your ass when you couldn't. I love you more and more each day. You are an amazing, beautiful woman, wife, mother, lover. Besides, I thought it was sexy as fuck."

My 'mother' began to dissipate, and her hard-nosed anger melted as my eyes began to well up with tears. Sometimes, I swear my mother's spirit took over my body when I was angry.

Why does he love me? I wondered as I stood up and wiped my tears, opening the door.

Standing before me, in all his smug-ass awesomeness with his arms open wide, my husband welcomed me. Me and all my stupid, temper tantrum, childish, spoiled ass baggage. I melted against his chest while his arms circle me, causing my heart to flip over as it always did when I was in his arms. Finally, I relaxed and let the tears flow. How did I get so damn lucky?

We stood wrapped in each other's arms for a few more minutes before he pushed me back to look into my eyes. A smug smile was tickling along his mouth, "So, that book ... you wouldn't want to share it, would you? I think Daddy's going to likey." He wiggled his eyebrows and smiled, taking me by the hand and led me to the couch where I left my Kindle. He picked it up and smiled once more. I was butter to his toast and followed him into our bedroom.

Alex led me to the bed, gesturing for me to climb in. I did as instructed and pulled myself to the headboard, where I propped myself up on the pillows and waited with bated breath.

He placed the Kindle on the bedside table, emptied his pockets, and put the contents beside it. Swiping his phone, he pulled up a song I hadn't heard in a long time, "*Only You*," sung by Travis Tritt. I remembered this was one of our favorites back in the day. I used to strip to it while he watched. Oh. My. God. He's stripping. His hips swayed to the rhythm as his fingers loosened his belt and lowered the zipper allowing his pants to fall to the floor. His manhood was bulging against his briefs, and my insides were jello. The song continued as he moved in smooth motions, slowly lowered his underwear, and freed his cock. It was hard as a fucking rock, and the tip glistened with precum. He wiggled his hips and turned, bending over, oh that gorgeous ass, his balls swayed between his legs. I can't wait any longer.

I sprang to the foot of the bed, reaching for him, but he backed away with a tsk, "A-a-a, no you don't, Kitten. I am going to be your Master and you, my sweet pussy ... cat." Pointing to the pillows, he ordered me, "Back to the pillows. Watch and wait. I'll give you permission when you can touch. I am in charge. You will listen and obey. And love every fucking minute of it! Is that understood?"

I popped my bottom lip out in a pout, hoping it would work and help me get what I wanted. Alex's rock-hard python of love. Looking up through my sad eyes, I batted my lashes in an attempt to convince Alex to give me what I wanted, but all it got me was a slap on my ass.

"Ouch!" I tucked my tail and crawled back to the head of the bed, like a good little pussycat, rubbing my bottom. Damn, that kind of turned me on.

Catch Me if You Can

"Beckee, you would not believe what Alex and I did yesterday," I giggled. "I read a bit from the book to him, and well, let's just say, damn!!" I breathed through the phone at my best friend. "The more I read, the more excited we both became. Before I knew it, he had turned off the TV and had me pinned under him. My lady bits are so tender this morning."

"I told you, didn't I?" she replies, "There's nothing like a 'sexual jump' to add fuel to your love life. We all need it now and again. You should go to an adult store together, too."

"An adult store? Do we have any in this neck of the woods?" I had heard about them but never been to one. There is one up north where my sister lives, and she's told me about going to it a few times. She's even had one of those 'Fantasy Parties'. I've always wanted to go to one just to see what it was all about, but I've never been invited. Hell, I don't even know if they have parties like that here.

"Yes, there's an adult store in Mitchville, just a twenty-minute drive from here. You should stop by and give it a look."

We talk a little longer before I realize I've been on the phone for over an hour and haven't done an ounce of housework. Tomorrow is Saturday, and I did not want to spend it cleaning and doing laundry. I needed to get my ass up and off the phone.

"Well, Beck, I've got to get my ass off here and get some work done. Thanks for the info; I'll look into it." Not!

Disconnecting the call, I realize just how empty and quiet the house is with everyone gone, and I have it all to myself. Instead of feeling melancholy, I blare music and sing along at the top of my lungs, dancing here and there as I work my way through the house, dusting, and vacuuming.

My mind occasionally drifts to my earlier conversation with Beckee, and the more I think about it, the more my curiosity wins out. I want to see what an adult store is all about. My insides flutter in excitement as I decide, yes, we are going to Mitchville. Now all I have to do is get the nerve to ask Alex.

Alex's a little late coming home, but that just gave me a little more time to concoct a plan. About an hour later, he walked through the door.

"Hey, babe," he leaned in and kissed me, "Mmmm, you smell delicious." My heart fluttered as he feathered my neck with soft kisses, wrapped his arms around my middle, and pulled me in tighter. I hummed in delight and cocked my head to the side to allow him more access.

Smiling, I asked, "How was your day?" Turning slowly in his arms so I could wrap my arms around his neck and return his kisses. My body instantly conformed to his, fitting perfectly, as though we were two puzzle pieces. Even after all these years, our body's shape was much different than when we first met. Gravity and menopause are not a woman's friend, more like her enemy. And I have cursed her for ten years now, ever since my thighs decided to meet and my tits decided to sag and fall, becoming part of my expanding waistline. Fucking bitch!

Alex pulled away and looked into my eyes, "Do you know how damn sexy you are in those shorts?" He cupped my bottom. "And this ass, it's mine. I have always been an ass man, but yours, baby, only gets better over time." He squeezed my ass cheeks, pulling me against him, his breath hot against my face as he whispered, "I have wanted you all damn day." He playfully slapped my ass, and a squeal rushed past my lips at the same time, my girlie bits felt the zing of pleasure.

Surprising myself, I pushed away from him and ran, "You have to catch me first, Daddy." I declared over my shoulder as I made my way to our bedroom and jumped on the bed. My body was singing with thousands of energy bolts, and I can't remember the last time I felt so turned on. Biting my lip, I turned to find him only a few steps behind me, the feral look burning in his eyes telling me he is as hot and horny as I was.

He reached for me, but I rolled out of his reach, giggling as I did. The air around us crackling with passion and something different, something I didn't recognize at first. But I soon realize what it was when he crossed the room, reaching for me once more, growling when I rolled away from him once again.

Fear! That's what's different. The excitement the fear brought, that he might punish me. My stomach flipped, and I felt the moisture pool in my panties. Holy hell, I wanted him to punish me.

I stood in the center of the bed, just out of his reach, another bonus to having a king-size bed.

His nostrils flared with each breath, his eyes turned darker, and the vein on the side of his neck pulsed faster. "You want Daddy to spank that ass of yours, don't you, babygirl." He stated, "When I get ahold of you, you're going to get just what you ask for." He stepped up on the ottoman at the foot of our bed and lunged for me, but it slipped, and he crashed his knee against the wooden footboard before falling onto the bed, just inches from me.

Unable to control myself, the room was filled with laughter. The look in his eyes when he wiped out was priceless. Tears danced along my eyelids as I laughed harder, hiccupping as I tried to compose myself, dropping to my knees and crawling over to my husband as he rolled in pain, clutching his knee. "Son of a bitch, that hurt."

I bit my lip to swallow the laughter still bubbling up, "Are you ok?" I giggled, trying in vain to look sincere.

Alex jerked his hand away from me and pouted, "What do you care? You were laughing at me. I was trying to get my groove on, and you laughed. I could have died, you know." He pouted, his voice that of a child, made the laughter explode as he reached for me. We lay on the bed, laughing at ourselves. He pulled me close, "I love you, babygirl." He declared, placing a tender kiss on my forehead, making my heart melt. How'd I get so damn lucky?

The Toy Store

Daddy was excited about this new adventurous lifestyle; it wasn't long until we had to make a trip.

"Where are we going?" I asked

He pointed and replied, "This way."

He knew I hated it when he did that, so he did it all the time.

We drove to the outskirts of town and hopped onto the interstate, and headed east. My mind began to wander to all the possible places he was taking us, and it wasn't long until I knew. And I was horrified.

We pulled up to the front of the store and parked. My eyes nearly bulged out of my head in disbelief. I turned to him as if in slow motion and said, "Hell no. I'm not going in there. People will know."

"So, what do you think they are doing in there? Come on, babygirl."

The insides of my belly started to quiver, and my limbs began to tingle. I knew he would not allow me to stay in the car, and if I were honest with myself, I was curious. And I definitely didn't trust him in there alone. So, I opened the door and stood on my jello legs, holding onto the door for fear I'd fall. Then, I took a deep breath and willed my legs to move.

Alex opened the door, and we were immediately overcome with the scents of sandalwood, lavender, and ylang-ylang. Suggestive music blared from the speakers, and we were greeted with a cheerful, "Welcome, can I help you find anything today?"

Looking up, I was mortified to see a young girl smiling back at me. I was shell-shocked. I have no idea what to say, so I just stare back at her, my mouth hanging open.

She winked at me, "Oh, first time, huh? Who is this handsome young man popping your cherry?"

Of course, Alex played that comment up, puffed up his shoulders, and sucked in his gut. "You can call me Daddy."

Her eyes widened, and she took a few steps back with no idea what to say to that, how to react or what to do. Now it was her turn to look like a fish out of water, and I kind of enjoyed it. Served her right, the cocky little tramp. What kind of mother allowed her young daughter to work in a place like this?

Alex took my hand and led me further into the store. Leaning down, he whispered, "That shut her up, didn't it?"

I don't know whether it was his statement or just having his warmth so close to me, but I felt my nerves begin to relax. Finally, I allowed myself to enjoy this new adventure with my husband.

We looked around the store, stopping in every department to inspect the products. He was determined that I get a sexy outfit. I was determined my fat ass and gut wouldn't fit nor be sexy in any of them. So, we agreed on stockings, a blindfold, and furry handcuffs. We put them in our basket and turned to go into the next area.

Holy shit! That's a big black dildo, and what the hell was a fist doing hanging beside it? Do people ... I gasp, "Women really use those things?"

Alex cocked his head, "I'd say any woman able to handle something like that would probably be a swamp moose, and my poor little 'peetie' wouldn't be able to hold a candle."

I rolled my eyes and continued to the more 'appropriate' items. There were vibrators of all colors and sizes. Some even had rechargeable batteries. There were anal beads, Ben Wa balls, "Oh, yeah, I want those." I told Alex, "I hear they are great to keep *her* in shape."

Nipple clamps, blow-up dolls, strap-ons, wands, movies, sex swings, whips, ball gags, the toys went on and on. And here we were, a middle-aged couple, one bald and the other gray foraging through the goods.

Alex made his way over to the bondage gear, and I stayed behind looking at a glass case with beautiful, yes, I said beautiful glass dildos. Wondering how anyone could actually use them. Beside them was another glass case with glass butt plugs with different décor. One had a huge ruby, while another had a rainbow tail, and yet another had a raccoon tail. There was an emerald, black, gold, and a pearl-ended one too. How the hell did you sit down with one of those in?

Alex walked over and asked, "You want one of these?"

I shot a look at him, and he laughed.

"I was actually thinking of getting one for you, Daddy." And walked off to my next display case. Bullets.

"Those are normally used for clit stimulation," The same young girl snuck up beside me, scaring me. I jumped, throwing the item in my hand. It bounced off a display case and landed against the wall, convulsing, its vibration echoing throughout the store.

I didn't say a word. I just tucked my chin and searched for Alex, ready to get the hell out of here.

"Are you done yet?" I asked, embarrassed.

"Yeah." Walking away from me, he stopped and looked back at me, and in a much louder voice, than needed, he announced to the store, "Babygirl, which of the Ben Wa balls did you want? The one with or without the string?"

I shot him a few daggers and looked around to see how many people were waiting for my answer, surprised to find no one paying us any mind. They were too busy picking out their new toys.

Walking over to him, I leaned in close, brushing my chest against his arm for added measure. Purring, "I'll take these."

We paid for our items and left.

"Where to now?" I asked.

"Walmart. I need a new rod and reel."

We pulled into the parking lot of Walmart, and I suddenly got a naughty, dirty idea and instantly decided to go for it. I reached for our toy bag and pulled out the Ben Wa balls.

"What are you doing with those?" he asked.

I said nothing and simply smiled while opening the package. I looked over at Alex, and his eyes were darkening, his nostrils began to flare, and I knew I had his attention. Licking my lips, I placed the balls in my mouth, and his eyes widen, and the act itself caused him to squirm in the seat as he kept watching. His action spurred my self-confidence, and the dirty girl hidden inside me came forward.

The balls were glistening with moisture as I pulled them slowly from my mouth and held the last one in my mouth as the other dangled. I dropped my hands to the waistline of my shorts and simultaneously lifted my bottom as I pulled down the fabric. Placing my heels on the dashboard, I spread my knees and inserted them, never taking my eyes off Alex as he squirmed and attempted to push down his erection.

"You are one naughty babygirl. Daddy is going to have to punish you when we get home."

Dearly Beloved

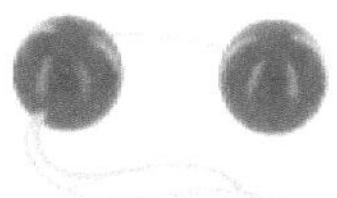

It was a beautiful fall afternoon, our daughter's childhood best friend was getting married, and we were attending the wedding. I wasn't one to wear dresses very often, so I only have a couple. That particular day, the naughty little girl inside me wanted to tease and play and see how far she could push her daddy.

The little black tank dress I chose fit me well without making my stomach look too big. It fell to the top of my knees, and my still sun-kissed skin looked pretty damn good. I finished my makeup and walked into the living room, where Alex waited. My stomach flip-flopped at his reaction, the burning in his eyes, and the passion that flowed between us. He walked over, lifted my chin with a finger, and kissed me, "You are beautiful."

My heart melted, and I blushed a little, "Thank you."

The wedding was about an hour's drive away. We relaxed and listened to some music on the way, reminiscing and walking down memory lane. Talking about the day we were married and the feelings that swarmed in each of us.

Finally, we arrived, and the venue was beautiful. It was a Baptist college, and the wedding was being held at the campus cathedral.

The vibrant colors and beautiful music stirred everybody's heart and emotions. The bride was beautiful, and the groom looked scared shitless. The ceremony was grand, and the bride's mother wiped away her tears as her husband escorted their daughter down the aisle. It was magical, and the aura within the room was palpable.

I looked over to Alex and smiled. The butterflies in my stomach fluttered happily. I crossed my legs and felt the sensation between my thighs. She was hungry, and she wanted to be naughty. I stifled the giggle that threatened to appear and squeezed my thighs tight in the hope of quelling the burn building there.

My patience was wearing thin, and finally, the minister announced the new couple, and we were dismissed to the fellowship hall across the way.

Alex took my hand, and we walked together down the sidewalk to the reception, no longer able to control myself. I leaned in and whispered, "I have a surprise for you, Daddy."

His brow cocked, and he looked at me. I can't help it; a sinister grin crossed my face.

"What is it, babygirl?"

I clamped my mouth shut and walked through the doors.

The dinner was delicious and the cake divine. We toasted the bride and groom and watched them as they took to the floor for their first dance. I excused myself and went to the restroom. I couldn't stand it any longer; my body was about to combust.

I pulled up my dress and sat on the toilet, proud of my achievement, now to get my plan in motion. Taking care of business, I emptied my bladder and wiped. Noticing the exposed pink loop hanging between my outer lips. I grabbed my phone and took a below the waist selfie and sent it to my husband. The vivid photo of my smooth, hairless vag with a pink loop hanging from within. Giggling as I stood and pulled my dress down. I stepped to the sink and washed my hands and checked my dress to make sure it was covering everything. Then suddenly, my phone lit up. It was him!

I ignored the continuous vibration as I made my way back to our table. Looking around, Alex wasn't there, and I asked our daughter where he had gone.

She replied, "He went looking for you."

I took my seat and crossed my legs, waiting patiently. I couldn't see Alex, but I could feel him. The sudden electrical current he always exuded surrounded me, and before I could turn to look, he had a fist full of my hair and was pulling me up from my seat. I wouldn't say it hurt, no it was exciting, causing a jolt of hot lava to my very core. He leaned in and demanded I follow him, and like a good babygirl, I obeyed.

We walked out the door and into a vestibule that seemed as though it were separated from the rest of the building, and within the vestibule were two doors. Men. Women.

Alex grabbed the closest doorknob, but it was locked. So, he grabbed the other door, and it opened freely. He stepped through and dragged me in behind.

It was a very small bathroom, one toilet and one sink, and barely enough room for your feet.

"Take them off." He ordered.

I looked at him sheepishly, "Take what off?"

A growl rolled from deep within him, and he snarled, "Your panties!"

The rebel inside me chose just that moment to appear, and she replied, "No. You do it."

His eyes were blazing with fire, and the heat within the tiny room became stifling. In one swift move, he turned me and lifted my dress above my hips.

The air rushed from his lungs, and he nipped at my ear. "You're not wearing any? You naughty, naughty girl."

I tilted my head to give him better access, and suddenly I was slammed against the sink, his pelvis hard against my ass, and an unexpected pain between my legs.

I cried out, and he quickly jerked away.

"I'm sorry, baby girl, I didn't mean to hurt you."

Taking a deep breath, I willed my vaginal muscles to relax as I reached between my legs and pulled out the balls that had just moments before ripped through my cervix. "I don't think there's room for him and these." I handed them to daddy. He smiled and popped them in his mouth, turning me once more, and drilled me from behind.

It was fierce, it was animalistic, and I fucking loved it. Daddy pulsed inside me and hissed, "You are a very naughty girl."

Suddenly there was a knock on the door, and our little fuckfest was over. I looked at Alex and whispered, "What are we going to do? We can't both come out of here. Whoever it is will know what we've been doing. I don't have panties to put on, and unless I can 'drain' my love tunnel, I'm going to have cum dripping from my coochie and down my legs."

Alex pulled up his slacks and placed the balls in his pockets, then grabbed a handful of toilet paper and shoved it between my thighs, "Problem solved." Before shrugging his shoulders and pulling my dress down, "Tell 'em to eat their heart out."

He opened the door and stepped out, greeted by a young man.

"Hi, be just a minute." He said without missing a beat. "Come on, babygirl."

We walked hand in hand back into the reception hall, and it felt like everyone's eyes were on us. Our daughter walked up to us and asked where we had been. I looked at her daddy, and he looked at me and smiled.

"*No*! You two didn't! Please tell me you two didn't just fuck in the church."

Neither of us said a word. We just shrugged our shoulders and walked out onto the dance floor.

Road Trip

It was a hot summer day, the birds were singing, and the sun peeked through the leaves as a gentle breeze blew. Alex woke me up with a slap to my bottom and ordered

me to get dressed. When I asked him where we're going, he shrugged his shoulders and replied, "Road trip."

Have I told anyone how much I hated and yet loved when he did this to me? I mean, sometimes, I just wanted to stay home, in my pajamas and in bed. And this just happened to be one of those days.

I gave in as I always did, and threw my blankets off, and grumbled under my breath, "Lord, I hope we aren't going far." I knew very well he'd never tell me if I asked, but there is one question he had learned to answer over the years, or else his plan hit a snag, and we both knew how much he hated that. But, he disappeared before I got a chance to ask it, so I grabbed my toothbrush and began scrubbing the morning funk from my mouth. Damn it.

I glanced in the mirror. Ugh, I looked like shit. My allergies were kicking my butt, and by the looks of the bags under my eyes, they knew about this road trip because they were fully packed.

I spat the last of the toothpaste into the sink as he walked back into our room, grabbing his phone, "You about ready?" he asked.

I was standing in my pajamas, and he has to ask if I was ready?

Throwing my hands up, I looked at him, "Yep, not wearing clothes today since you won't tell me where we're going." Without missing a beat, he shrugs his shoulders, turned, and replied, "Whatever you want," as he walked out of the room.

Well, crap, that didn't work. I slipped into a pair of shorts and a tank top, remembering I had yet to ask the one question he always answered and ended up being my only clue.

"Hey, should I go pee before we leave?" I shouted as I grabbed my flip-flops and waited for his answer.

"Yes!"

"Dang it," I whined to myself as I go to the bathroom. We weren't staying in town. "Where the hell is he dragging me today?" I grumbled.

Alex appeared in the doorway, "You'll have to wait and see," he answered, "Oh, and by the way, wear comfortable shoes." He ordered, turned, and disappeared.

We hit the road early, "Hell, I haven't even had my first cup of coffee," I complained. But Alex explained he would take care of that when we pulled into McD's and grabbed a coffee and a quick breakfast.

I settled in my seat with coffee in hand and conceded to the abduction, and decided to quit being such a party pooper. After all, this was what it was all about, right? Being in our, wait, what were these years called? It wasn't Golden Years; no, it couldn't be. We were too young. So, what was this period called? I let my mind wander as I tried to think of the right name for this period in our lives.

I was lost in my thoughts, and I didn't realize we had exited the interstate, now traveling on a two-lane state road. That was when Alex gave me my next clue. "Dial-up that fancy phone of yours and get the coordinates to Carthy Falls."

And for a moment I was dumbfounded. "Huh?"

"Carthy Falls, I thought it would be a nice place to spend the day. We've lived here our whole lives and never seen it. So, let's try something new. Dial it up, babygirl."

I did as instructed, and before long, we were turning into the National Park. It was beautiful. The leaves on the trees had begun to turn dry from the oppressive heat, and the stream that ribboned through the area was just a trickle. And it was absolutely breathtaking.

I felt like I was standing in the middle of a giant bowl. The boulders and cliffs surrounding the park were lined with native trees to our state. The artwork created by nature decorated each stone as though it were hand-painted, brilliant designs and colors. Some looked like sand, while others shimmered and sparkled like diamonds. It was simply gorgeous. The only sounds were that of the waterfall as we drew closer and the breeze as it blew through the leaves.

The air was hot and humid, and the muddy, musty scent of the waterfall filled our noses. Ahh, heaven on earth.

The hot July sun continued to barrel down on us as the sweat rolled down my forehead. And I was sure I looked like I'd pissed my shorts. I had a severe case of swamp ass. Yuck!

Alex took my hand as we walked along the path. His thumbs made swirls on top of my hand, filling my heart with joy and making me forget all about my discomfort. You see, it was the simple things he did that made me feel as though I could explode with love. It was then the word I was looking for hit me; just like the name of the path we were taking, so did the title of this time of our lives.

Seasoned.

As the path wound around the mature trees and native flowers, I got the feeling of contentment. Just being here with Alex, hell, being anywhere with him makes me happy. He completed me in every way, and for a moment, I wondered why he loved me? How did I get so damn lucky? Where would I be today without him? My eyes began to burn, and a painful lump formed in my throat, a tear tickled my cheek as it tumbled down the side of my face. But I wiped it away before Alex could see it, not wanting him worried about my crazy mood swings. Damn hormones.

The path was steep, and with the recent rains, I soon discovered it was slicker than snot.

Without warning, my shoe slipped, and I swore it was all I could do to keep from doing the splits. My right foot slid down the embankment, and my left followed suit. My hand flew up and grasped nothing but empty air. Alex reached for me but missed as my ass hit the ground. Hard.

Squish, my face drew up in disgust. The mud mushed up between my legs and around my ass, and my hands landed painfully beside my hips, "Aww, fuck." Mud splattered between my fingers, and I was stuck. Do I laugh, or do I cry? A nanosecond ticked by, and Alex decided for me as his laughter echoed through the trees.

I looked over my shoulder to see him bent over, laughing his ass off. Catching him off guard, I quickly jerked his hand down, and before he had time to think, he was flailing around like a fish on a bank. His arms were going in circles, and his feet slipped apart. He reached for the nearest tree branch, grasping it before he fell. The grin on his face quickly faded when the branch broke, and he slipped off the path and into the stream with a splash.

"Son of a bitch."

Now, it was me who's laughing my ass off. What a sight we must be. Me, sitting in mud at the bottom of the path, and my husband, slipping on the mossy rocks, splashing in the stream, surrounded by a cloud of muddy water.

I crawled to the nearest log and pulled myself up, my ass wet and slimy and my hands caked with mud.

"Come on in," Alex insisted. "The water feels great." Using his hands, he splashed me with water; I must admit, it did feel refreshing. So, with a squeal I jumped in and was instantly surrounded by a cloud of brown water.

The sun continued to beat down on us, scorching our exposed skin, but the water cooled us down. Alex wrapped his arms around me and pulled me against him. There in the middle of the park, we sat, with the water dancing around us. Alex began to nuzzle my neck and the electricity zipped through my body to my core. His hands cupped my breasts and began to knead them. I threw my head back and moaned when he pinched my nipples.

"Yes!" I moaned again and turned to face him. Our mouths connected, and we began to make out. Right there, in the middle of a stream, in the middle of a State Park, and I have never been more turned on in my life.

When the Mood Strikes

"Shhhhh, listen. Do you hear that?" I whispered.

"Yeah, it's my dick cheering me on."

I swatted at his hands and hissed, "Seriously, listen. I hear voices," panic rose in my voice. "Damn it. Someone's coming. They are going to see!" I pulled away and began the fight of getting my wet shorts to let go of my legs so I could pull them up. Alex, in the meantime, was still trying to get his shorts off his shoe.

"What are you doing?" I hissed, "You need to get your clothes on. They're getting closer; hurry."

Alex kicked his shorts off his shoe, catching them in midair, and grabbed my hand at the same time. "Come on." He ordered, turning and running through the middle of the stream. The water splashed so loud I was certain they could hear us. Slipping on moss-covered rocks, I lost my balance and began to fall, but Alex tightened his hold on me and kept me upright just as we rounded the bend in the creek and disappeared from view.

Stopping to catch my breath, I began to laugh, "I hope like hell no one saw us. With you running through the water holding your clothes while your tallywacker bounced about freely. Seriously, what if they saw and they called the police?"

Pulling me flush against his bare skin, "I hope they enjoyed what they saw. Now drop your pants and bend over."

Looking around, I nervously bit my lip. I mean, there are people out here just across the water from us.

Seeing my hesitation, Alex remarked, "Don't worry, no one can see us through all these cattails and nettles." In one swift motion, he turned me, jerked down my shorts before placing his hand between my shoulders, and bent me over. He gripped my hips and plunged inside me. I combust, spots appeared in front of my eyes before everything goes black, and I felt my knees begin to buckle. Alex tightened his fingers around my hips to keep me from falling, all while he was still pumping. Holy shit. Suddenly, I hear screaming, "Yes! Yes! Fuck me harder!" Alex growled in my ear, "Yes, baby, Daddy's going to give you what you want. Hold tight. This is going to be a load." He plunged one last time, biting at my shoulder as his body shivered, and that's all it took. I was spiraling out of control, riding the most extreme orgasm I'd ever had, or at least remembered. And I was pretty sure if I had an orgasm that intense, I would have remembered it.

The water swirled around our ankles, our bodies still connected. I was dizzy, hot, sweaty, my lady bits were tingling, and I needed a drink. I was going to pass out.

Slowly Alex pulled away from me and sat down in the water, pulling on my hand, "Come on, you look like you're going to faint. Get in here and let the water cool you off." He ordered.

I pulled away, "Eww no! I don't want any organisms or bugs swimming in my hoo-ha. I'll splash some water on me and cool down that way."

I splashed the water up onto my legs and worked my way upward. I have to admit, the water was refreshing, cooled my skin from both the sun and what we had just experienced. I had forgotten how exciting it was to have sex outside, a chance of someone catching you. And I allowed a smile to spread across my face.

"What are you grinning at?"

I shrugged my shoulders, "Just thinking how happy I am and how lucky I am to have you."

"Damn right you are, don't forget it either." He smiled.

As though the world had just stopped, we were surrounded by complete silence. The birds stopped singing, and the wind stopped blowing. The only sound was that of the water as it trickled over the rocks. It was surreal, tranquil, and perfect.

Alex slipped back into his shorts and held his hand out for me to take. "You want to stay or go get something to eat?"

That was a no-brainer; I was starving. "I could eat."

I took his hand, and he led the way up and out of the water, making sure I didn't slip as I climbed up the embankment.

We made our way back to the car. Thank God for our wet clothes. They kept us cool on the mile hike and were completely dry by the time we reached the car.

Hot, humid air hit me in my face when I opened the car door, and Alex knew there was no frickin' way I would sit in that smoldering heat. He reached in and started the car, and flipped the A/C on high. "It won't take too much time to cool off. You want me to get you a bottled water?"

He was too sweet. Damn, I was the luckiest gal in the world. I just smiled back at him and shook my head. The first thing I want to do is kick these damn shoes off. I hate wearing shoes; if my feet are hot, I was hot. And on top of hormonal hot flashes, I was about to blow my top. I toed off my tennis shoes and pulled off my socks, wiggling my toes as the air hit them. Ahh, yes, much better. Thankfully, I had brought a pair of my flip-flops and slipped them on my feet.

Alex reached over and took my hand. "Do you have any idea how much I love you?" Ending the question with a kiss to my hand and stealing my breath, I closed my eyes and savored this precious moment.

"You look tired. Why don't you lay back and take a nap? I'll wake you when we get someplace to eat."

He knew me all too well. I smiled at him, blowing him a kiss as I lowered the back of my seat and propped my feet up on the dash, closed my eyes, and drifted off to sleep as he sang along with Bruce Springsteen.

Proud Mary's

I felt my body shift as the car turned and decelerated as it came off the interstate. Alex laid his hand on my thigh, "Hey sweetheart, wake up. You hungry?"

I stretched and lowered my feet onto the floor, rising in my seat, as I rubbed the sleep from my eyes. Glancing out the window, nothing looked familiar to me, "Where are we?" I asked as I dropped the visor mirror and inspected my sleepy face and hair, trying to tame the unruly curls with my fingers. Slowing, we turned into a gravel parking lot, and I could hear live music coming from behind the building. We stepped out of the car and made our way up to the front, the door was held open by a metal doorstop and above the door, a sign read, 'Proud Mary's'. Instantly my mind started singing Tina Turner's *Proud Mary*, and my adrenalin started to pump; I fucking loved the place. Looking around, I took it all in. The interior reminded me of an old saloon. It was kinda dark. The walls were untreated wood, and the bar was made of cedar, with the walls dressed in the bark from cedar trees. It was gorgeous. And at each bar stool was a hook that hung from under the bar top for jackets and purses. The lighting was dusk; even though it was in the middle of the afternoon, the area was dank. At the end of the main room were five garage doors, opened to reveal a patio-style deck with steps that led down to a bottom patio that stepped out into sand and a volleyball net. On the far side of the volleyball court was another bar area stretching the length of the original building. It had a metal roof; but other than that, it was all open and reminded me of a beach bar. Behind it stretched the river, the murky green water drifted lazily as tied-up boats bobbed up and down in the wake of a passing jet ski.

"1 2 3," and a guitar riff surrounded us. I looked to the right and saw a stage set up and a band warming up for the night's show. "I flove this place!" I announced as the hostess seated us on the patio.

Our server stopped at our table to get our drink order. Alex asked, "Do you want a margarita?" I glanced at the menu, "Yes, a mango margarita, please. And a glass of water with lemon." She nodded and walked away.

It was hot, the humidity was stifling, and the air was literally clinging to me. I was thirsty and couldn't wait to get a long hard pull on my frozen margarita, and just like that, it was sitting in front of me. The beautiful orange color, the sweet scent, and the frosty fog was dancing around the glass. I lifted it to my mouth and closed my lips over the straw, and with one suck, I am in heavenly bliss. The mango slushy cooled me as it traveled down the back of my throat, the tequila mixed with the sweetness added to the addictive flavor. I couldn't seem to stop.

"You might want to slow down there," Alex warned. "You remember what tequila did to you last time."

I do remember, it was awful! I had never been so sick in my life. But that was from taking shots. This was different, it was in a mixed drink, and I was eating with it. So, it was all good. Right?

Wrong!!!

It was so damn hot that I ended up sucking that frozen margarita down fast along with numerous brain freezes. But damn, it tasted good.

We started out sitting under an umbrella, but as the afternoon went by, the sun shifted and soon shone down on me. It wasn't long before I started feeling the effects of the sun and alcohol mix. Looking over to Alex, "I think we need to head on home. I was really feeling fuzzy now, and this heat is only making it worse."

Alex looked at me and gave that devilish smile, "I told you. Come on, Daddy will get you home and into bed."

I shot him a glare, *smart ass* and rose from my chair. Damn, it was getting hotter by the minute. What the hell is going on? I grabbed my glass of water and chugged it, placing the empty glass on the table as Alex motioned for me to take the deck stairs down and to the car. So, I did as instructed. Down the steps, across the lower deck, and back up another set of stairs. Alex reached for my hand, "No, sweetheart, we don't want to go back up. We want to go to the parking lot. You know where I parked the car?"

In my defense, I had no idea there were two sets of stairs coming off the patio we were just on. How was I to know the steps didn't lead to the parking lot?

Alex took my hand and led me around the volleyball court and down the sidewalk.

"Hey," a voice drew our attention. "How about entering our contest to win Carrie Underwood tickets."

Well, hell yeah! I love Carrie Underwood. I stepped up to the tent where the men stood, "What do I have to do?"

"Just fill this out, and we'll put you in for the drawing." One of them instructed.

I took the paper and began filling it out.

Name: Lisa Collins

Phone: 354-328-3425.

Watching over my shoulder, Alex laughed and took the slip off the table. "Umm, babygirl, 3425? That's not your number."

Oh, shit! It wasn't. Where the hell did I get that? I scribbled through the last four digits and added the correct ones, smiled up at the gentlemen, and shrugged my shoulders, "I guess the sun and margaritas messed with my head."

Surprise

The workday went by rather smoothly, thank God. I actually had some energy left. Perhaps I'd surprise Alex when he got home. A devilish smile spread across my face as a plan formed in my naughty mind.

Masey met me at the door, ready to go potty. I let her out, dropped my purse and lunch box on the table before turning and following after her outside. I sat on the porch swing as I waited for Masey to do her 'deed'. It was still sweltering, but occasionally, a cool breeze blew, so I decided to enjoy a few minutes on the porch swing.

Swinging back and forth, I got lost in my imagination and the naughty plan forming. The more I thought about it, the more turned on I became, and the more I convinced myself that it was a fan-fucking-tastic plan. Excitement boiled deep in my belly, and my decision was made.

Masey startled me as she came running around the side of the house and up on the porch like something was hot on her tail. She had that guilty look on her face, but she tried to hide it with a swoosh of her tail, and I swore she was wearing a shit-eating grin.

I reached down and rubbed behind her ears, "What have you been into, young lady?" She answered with a thump thump thump of her tail and a bark. "Come on, girl, let's go in. Mommy has something special planned for daddy."

I gave Masey a dog treat, and she happily hopped onto the couch and began to chew. That would keep her busy for a while and out from under my feet. I headed into the bedroom, put fresh linens on the bed and spritzed the pillows with vanilla body spray. I checked the time, 4:50. Happy to find I still had time for a shower and to freshen my makeup. As I removed my clothes, I realized my legs were stubby. If I were honest with myself, Alex couldn't care less about the hair on my legs. But I wanted everything to be perfect, so I opted for a bath instead to shave all my girly parts smooth.

Setting the timer on my phone so I didn't lose track of time, I stepped into the bath and sank into the rich, thick bubbles. Ahhh, heaven. Laying back, I enjoyed the calming warmth, and before I knew it, the timer was going off, and I realized I hadn't shaved or washed anything. Water splashed out onto the floor as I quickly sat up in the tub and began to take care of business.

Stepping out of the tub, I toweled off and slathered my smooth skin with the lotion Alex had gifted me for Christmas. Wanting to do something a little different, I decided to wear a sweater. The crocheted design was very revealing, so I decided not to wear anything beneath, and it fell just at my hips, revealing my smooth lower lips and my thighs. I slipped on my black thigh-high stockings and freshened my makeup. Making sure I wore my 'fuck me' red lipstick.

I checked my reflection in the mirror, pleased with what I saw, and glanced at the time, almost time for Alex to walk through the door. The butterflies that had been dormant for years spring to life and took flight in my stomach. I made my way to our bed, and something out of the corner of my eye caught my attention. As if in slow motion, as though a sexy, sensual seductress had taken over my body, I reached for the scarf hanging from my dresser mirror. It belonged to my late mother-in-law, it was unique, and that was why I decided to keep it. The silky material was cool and smooth to my hand as I carried it over to the bed. I carefully positioned myself in the center of our bed, making sure my sweater revealed just enough to entice Alex, make his blood pump fast and him hard. I used three pillows, fluffing them before I propped myself up and began to tie my wrists together with the scarf. It wasn't easy, but after a few tries, I finally accomplished the look I was going for, and just in time.

I heard the sound of a car door slam and straightened my shoulders, licked my teeth, and placed a pout on my lips, bent one knee before I lifted my bound wrists above my head in a submissive position. Oh, good lord, I didn't know what was more exciting, the butterflies in my stomach or my twat box. They were both tingling.

The door opened, I heard footsteps. They were getting closer, and I could tell by the sound he was headed toward the kitchen. Doing my very best to look sexy, I slowly turned my head to watch for him.

Oh shit! My mouth dried instantly, and the butterflies fall dead to the pit of my stomach, and my girly parts are completely mortified. You see, it wasn't Alex standing in my living room, in front of my open bedroom door, but our daughter's boyfriend, Rick!

Thank the sex gods, he went straight through the house and didn't stop and look into my room.

OMG! What the holy hell is he even doing here? I grabbed the corner of the comforter and covered myself as best I could with my fucking hands tied together. Of course, if it could happen, it would happen to me. Damn it. I willed myself to disappear.

Rick's footfalls were coming back through the house, getting closer to my room. I shoved my hands under the blanket and closed my eyes, pretending to be napping.

He stopped at my door, "You awake?"

I froze. I mean it, I didn't even breathe. All I could do was pray silently, God, please don't let him see me. I am so embarrassed. I promise I will never do anything this stupid again. Please, oh please, oh please.

He waited a few seconds while I waited an eternity before he turned and left. I heard the door close and strained my ears, making sure he's left before I open my eyes and look. Hell, for all I know, he did see me, and he knows I wasn't asleep. He was probably standing there waiting to catch me. Fuck. Fuck. Fuck. Fuck.

I wait a minute or two, just to make sure. I've convinced myself he's actually gone, and I opened my eyes. Yep. He's gone, and now I was alone, with my wrists bound, in black thigh highs. With my bare pussy shining for anyone to see.

That's it. I attempted to throw the comforter off me, which happened to be very difficult when your hands were tied. I ended up using my feet and legs and kicked the covers to the foot of the bed. I twisted my wrists around, trying to untie them, getting discouraged and pissed by the minute. One would think, if I could tie my hands together, I'd be able to untie them, right? Wrong! Fuck!!

Just then, I heard the door open and close. Fear swelled inside me, and I fought to get the blanket back over me. Shit shit shit shit shit! This whole damn thing had become nothing but a clusterfuck. I continue to stretch my legs out, trying to grasp the blanket with my feet, when the footfalls stop in front of the bedroom door and tears swell in my eyes. I stopped breathing and willed myself to disappear, trying to cover myself with my bound hands. I'd lost all my dignity and refused to look in the direction of the person standing there.

A slow whistle and hum pricked my ears, and the steps moved closer. "Mmmm. What do we have here?"

My eyes popped open, surprised to find Alex standing at the foot of our bed. His eyes blazed with lust and helped ease my embarrassment, but it was the devilish grin on his face that made me lose it.

I raised my hands and held them out toward him. My bottom lip was quivering, "I can't get 'em untied." I cried. "Help."

Smiling from ear to ear, he stepped around and stood beside the bed. His smoldering eyes raked slowly over me, from the fuck me red lips I was still sporting to my chest and the hard peaks of my nipples that protruded through the crocheted yarn. Further and further, his eyes roamed, stopping at the edge of my sweater, where it rested at the center of my velvet lips. His eyes widened, his pupils darkened as his tongue slipped out of his mouth, and the air escaped his lungs with a deep growl.

The feral look upon his face made all the thoughts and doubts of only a few moments completely escape my mind, replaced with a burning itch that I needed scratched. Now!

His eyes began perusing me again, down my stocking-covered legs and back up to my bound wrists. My stomach clenched while my lady bits fluttered, the moisture building, collecting. I fought the urge to squeeze my thighs together. I was desperate, on fire, and damn it, by the look in his eyes, we were about to burn the house down. Wait, had I paid the house insurance?

The thought quickly leaves my mind as I watched as the wheels began to turn inside his head. The look on his face revealed nothing. I haven't a clue what he's thinking. The silence was killing me. If it weren't for the passion burning in his eyes, I would think he wasn't impressed with my attempt.

The butterflies in my stomach came to life, and I held my breath as he began to trace my jaw with his finger. Down my neck and between my breasts, stopping at the edge of my sweater. Slowly his finger swirled, gently, just a whisper of a touch on my skin. Dipping it just enough between my folds and finding the bundle of nerves that rested there.

His brows raised seductively, and a grin spread across his face when his fingertip meets with my warm silky cream.

The sunrise filled our room with a warm glow. I stretched as far as my muscles would allow and reminded me I wasn't as young as I once was. The delicious ache between my thighs reminded me of the magical night spent all over the house. I slowly opened my eyes to find Alex watching me. The love in his eyes does me in. How'd I get so damn lucky? I squeezed my thighs together as the memory of last night filled my mind. Ouch, I winced.

"My girlie parts are gloriously tender." I smiled.

"Good! I wanted you to know I had been there." He winked.

An Audience

Friday nights had always been our date night, and this time we went to Red Lobster. The food, as usual, was scrumptious, and I decided to have a few drinks. Now ask any of my friends and family, they will tell you I was a lightweight. It has never taken much to make me tipsy. With that being said, after I consumed the two Sex on the Beach cocktails, my body was feeling warm, and I was very giggly.

It was dark when we got home, the summer night was humid, but we had the A/C blowing in the car. I was still warm, giggly, and horny as hell. Alex put the car in park and reached to turn the key, and that's when I went in for the kill.

I lunged across the console and gripped his manhood. "I want to suck your cock, now!" I declared as my tipsy fingers fought to unbelt him and loosen his pants. He didn't argue or put up a fight. Hell, no! His left hand slid down his side, and suddenly his seat moved, and the back reclined, making more room to maneuver. The seat stops, and he lifted his arms above his head and settled into his seat as if to say, 'have at it biatch'.

His reaction elicited a giggle from me as I leaned over him, but there was no way in hell I could reach. My body wasn't as limber as it once was. Shit. The light bulb in my drunken mind goes off, and I opened the door. The darkness was swallowed by the illumination of the dome light, and that idea went out the window. Damn it. I quickly closed the door and pulled my feet up in my seat to sit on my knees; that should do it. Now I had plenty of room to move about over the console. The inside of my belly danced in anticipation. It was like a drug to me. I had to have him, the power and control over him, especially when he was at my mercy. Yes!

His body swelled, and his breathing quickened. God, I hope he's close. My jaws were about to fall off. I revved up my speed and gave his nuts a good pull as I growled. That did it. His body tensed, and I felt the first pulse, and hot thick lava exploded in my mouth. He quivered beneath me, and his body slumped, "Damn, babygirl. You give the best head." I smiled and raised up, sitting proud as a peacock.

"I need a drink." I declared as he fastened his shorts. Grabbing my purse, I opened my door and stepped out of the car, looking up at the starry night. Hell yeah! I strutted my stuff up the sidewalk and into the house.

I grabbed a glass of tea and headed for our bedroom, suddenly worn out by my extracurricular activity. I was too tired to change into my jammies, so I unfastened my bra and slipped it off and out through the armhole, tossing it on the dresser before climbing into our bed. He crawled in beside me and leaned over, and kissed me tenderly, "That was amazing."

I smiled back at him, "I love you, Daddy." Settling my head against his shoulder as the front door opened.

Laughter follows, and a few, 'Way to go, mom' gets tossed in for good measure. What the hell?

Our youngest walked into our room. This child has no filter. Hell, who am I kidding, neither of our girls has a filter.

"Hey, next time you want to 'rock dad's world' in the drive, make sure no one else is around."

My head snapped up off his shoulder, and my mind scrambled to find purchase. Wait, what?

"Rick and I were sitting in the car smoking a blunt when you pulled into the drive." She giggled again, "Then we saw your head disappear ..." She laughs out loud, "Bom-chicka- bow-wow."

A Picture's Worth

I was minding my own business this morning, sitting before the easel, and working on a new painting when my phone pinged with a text message.

MOM!!! Next time daddy takes pics of you, would you please make sure he puts them in a damn folder!

WTF are you talking about?

Daddy fucked up his phone and asked me to fix it. While I was scrolling through, freeing up some space. I got a full shot of your 'kooka'. And I'm not talking just a pic ... the fucking thing was posing! I will never be the same.

Don't be a hater.

The Night Sex Should've Sent Me to the ER

Daddy decided it was time for a 'special session'. He reached under the bed and brought out our toy case. No, seriously, we have a toy case. I was hoping one day to have my very own 'Red Room of Pain'.

He gave the order to get naked, nothing but my stockings. Of course, I complied with giggled anticipation.

I watched with bated breath as he pulls out leather cuffs and a blindfold. My excitement grew as he bound my wrists behind me and flipped me over onto my stomach before blindfolding me.

I listened intently as he stood behind me, pulling different items from our toy case, trying to guess what he'd chosen. The bed dipped under his weight, and I suddenly felt the warmth from his body as it hovered above me.

He began trailing wet kisses along my neck, nipping at my fevered skin.

"Yes!" I moan as the heat stirs in my chest, moving down into my nether region. I can feel myself grow wetter as his heat suddenly leaves me. Wait! Where did you go?

"Rise up on your knees," he ordered.

I struggled to raise my ass up off the bed. After all, my hands are fastened behind my back, and I wasn't as limber as I once was. A sudden fire erupted on my ass cheeks as a slap echoed through our room. "Ahhh." I cry out, not in pain but heated desire. *More* my body screamed as I wiggle my bottom, begging him. Slap! Another hot flash seared my skin. "Yes! Daddy, yes!"

His hand slipped beneath me, instantly finding the bundle of nerves hidden beneath my folds. An electrode zaps through me, and my ass raised off the bed of its own volition. He leaned down and hissed a warning. "When I tell you to get on your knees, I fucking expect you to obey, is that understood?" He was trying so hard to sound authoritative and all alpha. I can't help it; I lose it. I opened my mouth to say, 'Yes, sir,' but instead, a giggle erupted and turned into a full-blown laugh. Oh hell, this was not going to be good.

Within a millisecond, he'd flipped me over, my breath caught, and my lungs began to burn. He ripped the blindfold from my eyes, but my wrists were still bound and began to hurt under my weight, but I will not say it. I will not renounce. I will not say banana! (Our safe word)

I blinked a few times until Daddy came into focus. And there he stood before me in all his alpha splendor. The hair on his chest still glistened with water from his shower moments ago. My eyes traveled along every inch of him. From the top of his head down his neck, across his wide shoulders down to his fingers. God, how I love his calloused hands. The way they felt against my skin, their strength, their comfort. My heart swells.

I swallowed the lump forming in my throat and continued my walk along his body. It wasn't muscular and fit, per se, but it was mine. All mine. I have watched him grow and his body change over time, just as he has me. And loved him more every day. The gray in his facial hair, damn, it was hot. He was like fine wine. My eyes dropped to his manhood, and there he stood. Pointed straight at me like a compass pointing north. I bite my lip in anticipation as the heat pooled between my thighs.

Before my eyes could travel back up to his, like a lightning flash, he had grabbed my ankles and pulled me to the edge of the bed. In one swift motion, he had me bent in half, my knees pinned to my chest, and he was buried deep inside me. Oh, the magnificent glory of it all. He stood still, his thighs plastered against my ass, as his eyes darkened to a smokey gray. His pupils are blown with lust and desire, and then he finally began to move. Slowly at first but picked up speed as he thrashed deeper and deeper. Yes! I couldn't tell where he ended, and I began. We were one.

Alex wiggled his hips burrowing deeper still. Grabbing my feet, he pushed my knees further apart, and at this point, I was certain they are about to meet my chin. My lungs burned, an inferno raged through them as they screamed for oxygen. He continued to drive into me, deeper and harder.

"Make some fucking noise!" he yelled, thrashing harder and harder.

I wanted to, I really did. I loved the feral look he got when I talked dirty to him, and I tried, but it was impossible. Alex had me bent like a pretzel, my chin nearly pressed against my pussy, my arms pinned behind me. Oh God, I can't breathe! I was going to die. H was going to fucking kill me. What would he tell the kids?

9 1 1 What is Your Emergency

It was a beautiful morning, and the sun was shining. I could hear the waves of the ocean crashing against the sandy beach. I couldn't wait to get out there. Just the two of us.

With sunscreen and water in hand, I followed the sound of the crashing waves.

It was late in the season, not a soul for miles. We had the whole beach to ourselves. Alex had gone out before me to 'stake a claim'. He had set up a tent, far enough away from the water that our belongings wouldn't get wet. Beneath it was two chairs, a cooler, and my sexy man waiting for me.

We basked in the sunshine and napped in the shade while a constant breeze from the ocean kept us cool. We strolled out into the water, splashing in the waves and collecting seashells. But the best part was the sunset. The brilliant colors painted across the sky reflected off the water set the mood perfectly.

Of course, if you were to ask my husband about sex, he would say, and I quote, "Anytime the wind blows."

I was starting to feel the effects of my sun-kissed skin and the frozen margarita I had gulped down previously. My skin prickled as an electric current zapped through me, turning my insides to jello. My girly parts began to tingle, and my hands flew to my breasts, clutching and squeezing. Alex's eyes widened, and he squirmed in his chair. Oh yeah, I pinched and pulled my nipples as I watched him, and I know I've got him.

Alex kicked the sand as he stood and crossed the small space between us as he jerked his swim trunks down to his knees. He leaned down, pulling me to my feet and hard against him. "You've started something now, baby girl." He hissed as he dipped his head down, nipping at my neck and untying my top, letting it fall to the sand.

Before I knew it, we were spread out on the beach, my legs parted, my head thrown back in ecstasy.

The night was magical, every girl's dream of making love on the beach. The music of the waves lapping along the shore, the salty sea air mingling with my salty perspiration, and the breeze blowing in off the water, cooling my scorched skin. Nothing else mattered, just the two of us. We got lost in the moment, and before we knew it, the wind had shifted, and a storm had formed. We sat and watched the lightning dance across the sky, its forks glistening reflections on the ocean. Then, a sudden flash and explosion of light surround us as the lightning and water meet, the ground shook, and the thunder rolled.

"Time to go," Alex announced, grabbing his trunks and shimmying into them. I grabbed my cover-up and tossed it over my head just as the clouds erupted. We left the tent and chairs and ran toward the beach house. The sting of the blowing sand as it pelted our skin was like needles flying into us. We ran as fast as one could on dry sand, slipping a few times as the lightning split the sky above us.

Finally, we made it across the road and to our quaint beach bungalow. My eyes burned, and my teeth were gritty, full of sand. I needed a shower desperately. Stripping off what little covering I had, I stepped into the shower. Standing beneath the warm spray, feeling the layers of sand cascading down my body. I reached for my bath gel and loofah and began to scrub. I quickly discovered that was the wrong thing to do. My skin felt as though I was slicing it off in filets. I dropped the loofah to the shower floor and gently used my hands to wash, it wasn't much better, but at least it was bearable. That is until it was time to wash my cooter. I let out a blood-curdling scream that had Alex appearing out of nowhere.

"What's the matter?" he asked breathlessly.

I somehow got soap in my eyes, and they were burning like fire. But that wasn't the reason I screamed and trying to convey that to Alex while he's trying to rinse my eyes was not easy. I was in a lot of pain. I mean fucking intense, and I was crying hysterically.

My lip trembled, and I hiccupped, "Ccalll...9..9...1..1!" I managed to get out finally.

Now my Alex is a fantastic husband. After thirty-some years together, he had learned not to question me when I was in this state. Mind you, it was very few, and far between that I was hysterical, but when I was, it was normally justified.

Alex drops the washcloth and rushes to his cell. Quickly dialing 911.

"9 1 1, what is your emergency?"

"It's my wife; she's in a lot of pain. She told me to call you."

"What kind of pain? Where is she hurting? Is it her chest? Her head?"

"I don't know. I don't know." He rushed back into the bathroom, where I continue to cry. However, now I was standing in the middle of the shower, my knees bent and my pelvic thrust toward the spray. My hands were between my legs, trying to pull my labia apart, my outer lips open. But it wasn't helping. The shower spray kept hitting my 'peter pouch', as Alex called it, instead of where I needed it to.

"Baby, I got 911 on the phone. She needs to know where the pain is. Where are you hurting? What's wrong?" The worry in his voice was just so sweet.

With snot running down onto my lip, I sniffed and cried out, "My hoo-ha, there's sand in it!! I can't get it out!"

Alex said nothing, just stood there with his phone in his hand, looking at me as though I had three fucking heads. The look on his face. I couldn't even describe it. Horror? Distress? Confusion? Embarrassment?

A faint sound came through the phone, it was muffled at first, but when Alex hit the speaker, it became very clear.

Pure evil stares back at me, and for a moment, I was scared. But then I was over it. I mean, it was Alex. He doesn't have an evil bone in his body, and I am his baby girl. I was in a lot of pain and was scared. What if we couldn't get this shit out?

He disconnected the call and tossed his phone onto the vanity. The muscles in his temples start working, I could see his tongue moving on the inside of his cheek, and he began to rock back on his heels, staring at me.

Shit, he's really pissed. And then I got pissed. It was his fucking idea to screw on the beach. Not mine! How dare he get mad at me. I didn't do shit. This was his fault! And I chose that precise time to inform him.

"What? Why are you glaring at me? This is your fault! Not mine!"

"I called 911 ..." He reminded me, "I called 911 ..."

"It's not my fault!" I declared in my defense. I was in a lot of pain. You try having thousands of thousands of teeny tiny grains of glassy sand up your itty-bitty hole and see how you react.

It wasn't fun!!

July 4th

Damn, the sun was scorching, but what did one expect on the Fourth of July? I slathered myself with sunscreen. Ok, ok, maybe it wasn't SPF 50, and maybe the label read *Brown Biscuit*, but it did have SPF 4, so there was that.

I turned to my hubby, and with my seductive voice, "Oh, Daddy," I fluttered my eyelashes, "Could you please put lotion on my back and make sure the backs of my thighs are covered, you sexy beast."

My comment caused his blue eyes to turn the shade of gray, the color they always turned when he was horny.

He strolled up to me, his eyes smoldering, and took the bottle from my hand. "I'll lotion anything you want, baby girl." His voice and innuendo always made the butterflies in my stomach stir, even after all these years.

"Behave," I swatted at him playfully, "We have to be good." Ever since the kids had moved out, my husband had found his libido was just as potent as it had been when we were teens. I wasn't complaining, mind you, but we were at his sister's house, and there were dozens of people here. The pool was packed with kids splashing and playing. Jimmy Buffet was playing on the sound system, and the scent of beer and cigarettes floated through the air.

"Hey, Pop," our son yelled across the pool, "Would you bring me one of those German beers from the cooler?"

"You know they are better at room temp? That's how they drink 'em in Germany." I informed him.

"Yeah, well, they lost WWII, so that's how smart those fuckers are." He shot back.

I just shook my head. That's my boy, just like his daddy, a smart ass. I grabbed him a beer and took it over to him.

"Thanks, Ma," he popped the cap and chugged.

Shaking my head, I turned and jumped into the pool and grabbed a noodle to float. I kicked my legs and headed straight for the sexiest man in the pool. He was set up in the corner of the pool, cigar in hand, with a glass of tea sitting on the edge of the pool, within his reach. His little piece of heaven.

As I floated closer, he opened his arms and pulled me in, our bellies touching. He placed one of his legs between mine, spreading my thighs open, and the look in his eyes said it all. He slipped his hand between us and down to the center of my body. Instantly a zip goes through me as his thumb pressed against my clit.

My eyes widened, and I sucked in a deep breath, "Ohhhh."

I tried to push away from him, "Stop," I hissed, "Someone will see."

He pulled me closer. I should be surprised, but I wasn't when I felt his massive python of love pressed against me, and he ordered, "Be still!"

Before I knew it, he'd turned me around and tried to get my bathing suit bottom moved to the side. Again, I try to pull away, "Stop! We can't fuck in your sister's pool. Your floaties will be everywhere."

He leaned in, pressed his lips against my ear, his breath hot against my skin, "Go to the pool house, wait for me there." Followed with a pinch to my ass. "Mrs. Robinson."

"Ouch!" I jumped, "Yes, Sir." And scrambled out of the pool rubbing my ass, *Mrs. Robinson?*

Making my way into the pool house, I glanced around to make sure no one saw me and step through the door. The butterflies in my tummy had taken flight, and the anticipation was building. Looking around the glass building, I quickly realized there was nowhere to hide. "Well, if this isn't a cock block." I turn quickly as the door behind me suddenly opened.

In strolled the brother-in-law, "Hey, what are you doing in here?" His brows raised as he waited for my answer.

My brain decided right at that moment to take a vacation, and nothing came to mind. No excuse. No lie. I was busted. I stammered for a few seconds and opened my mouth to answer just as the door opened again and Alex rushed through.

Without looking up, he announced, "Your pool boy is here." Then, grabbed his junk, "And ready to fuck!" His eyes landed on the bro-in-law, then me, and he lifts his brow, smiled, and said, "Hey, wanna another beer?" That was all it took. The bro-in-law nodded his head and made his way to the cooler as though he had forgotten everything else.

Memories

It was another warm summer evening. We had been out on another one of Alex's road trip adventures, and I was exhausted. On the other hand, Alex was still wired for sound and looking for something else to get into.

The sun was setting, disappearing behind the trees along the western horizon. The breeze blowing through the windows now had a little bite to it as the temperatures dropped.

Slowing, Alex turns onto the off-ramp of the interstate that led to our hometown, but instead of turning right, he turned left.

"Where are we going?"

"You'll see."

We traveled down the highway for a while before turning off onto an industrial park road. Memories began to flood my mind, and the scents of honeysuckle and bourbon mash mingling in the air draw me away from the present.

The air was sticky, our skin covered in perspiration. The night sky was dark as ink, and the only light is that of the stars and the occasional lightning bug flitting by. The only sound for miles, coming from the crickets hidden in the tall grass, and every once in a while, a moan would escape and roll from deep within my throat.

Our clothes lay in a heap on the floorboard of his blue, two-wheel-drive Toyota pick-up, standard shift. If I had a quarter for every time that damn shifter got in our way.

We were getting it on, hot and heavy, when lights blind me. Alex stopped in mid-thrust and sat down behind the wheel. I squeal and dove for the floorboard (yeah, back in those days, I could fit), grabbing the blanket he always kept behind the bench seat of the truck.

A monster truck had come down the same country lane we had and was getting closer. Alex just sat in the seat, watching to see what they were going to do. It wasn't like we could go anywhere; they had us blocked in.

The truck kept coming closer, and I could hear the gravel beneath the giant tires crunch as they drew closer, stopping before they backed up onto a hill of gravel that we were parked behind. Shit, they can see down into our truck. I remain still, covered up with the blanket, so they don't see my itty-bitty titties. Alex cursed and pushed in the clutch, starting the truck. He then picked up his baseball cap and put it on top of his head. Dropping his hand down, he clutched the stick and shoved it into first gear, and pulled out from what was once our sacred hiding place.

We drove in complete silence down the gravel road out onto the main highway, both of us naked as a jaybird. Me, curled up in a fetal position on the floor and Alex behind the wheel, wearing his ball cap as though nothing had ever happened. Lord, if the cops were to pull us over ...

Blue Light Special

"What are we doing here?" I asked as we came to a stop along a tree line. The area had just been cleared and set for building.

Alex shut off the engine and swiveled in his seat, "What's it look like we're doing?" Reaching across the space between us, he attempted to pull me close but was unsuccessful. The console between us was in the way, and neither of us was as thin as we were back then.

"Come on," Alex instructed as he opened his door and got out, crawling into the back seat. It was a bench seat and should be much easier, right?

I don't waste any time swinging my door open and hustled my ass through the back door.

Alex was sitting proud as a peacock with his shorts around his ankles, his cock strutting with each tug of the fabric as he tried to get them off over his shoes. I gathered my shirt and ripped it over my head, dropping my shorts and thong on the ground before climbing in.

We don't waste any time. We are like two teenagers in heat, his hands and mouth are all over me, and I just can't get enough. My hands and mouth mimic his. My skin is on fire, and my girlie bits are wet and ready. Alex hooked his hands around my hips and lifted me off the seat, pulling me flush against his erection. From this angle, I knew it would be epic, and I could hardly contain myself.

"Hurry!" I demanded.

He plunged into me hard and fast, and it wasn't long before I felt the first wave building. I was so close.

In. Out. Thrust. Pull. Harder. Faster. Slower. Swirl.

The air inside the car was stifling, and the windows were covered in fog. It can't get much better than this.

Tap. Tap. Tap.

Alex jerked away from me, hitting his head on the roof of the car.

"Son of a bitch."

The sudden void of his body from mine left goosebumps covering my body as the sound returns.

Tap. Tap. Tap.

"Oh shit! Someone's out there!"

The sickening feel of déjà vu consumed me, and it was all I can do not to throw up. There was no blanket for me to hide beneath this time, and my panties and shorts were laying outside the door.

Alex quickly gave me his shirt to cover up with while he grabbed his shorts.

My heart was racing, and the veins in my neck are surely pulsing, "What are we going to do?" I whispered.

Alex looked at me, sweat pouring off his sleek bald head, "I don't know. We're stuck in the back seat. I can't drive off like the last time."

Suddenly a bright light shone in the window, glistening off the sweat-covered pane. "Police, open up."

Cops!

After all these years, and the numerous times and daring places we went parking during our youth, we never got caught by the law. And now, here we are, middle-aged, fat in some places, saggy in others, butt ass naked, and the cops found us. How in the hell are we going to explain this?

Wardrobe Malfunction

It was cold, the snow was blowing outside, but the water in the hot tub is gloriously hot, and the two together make for a perfect evening. Alex stepped in and slowly lowered himself down into the tub. I sighed in pure bliss as the water raised up and over my breasts, and Alex settled himself in the tub. Perfection.

He got settled across from me and smiled at me, "Do you know how much I love you?" he asked.

Just the sentiment and passion showing through his eyes warmed my soul, and I fall in love all over again.

"Do you remember the first time you told me you loved me?" I asked him.

He pondered my question for a few moments, and I turn myself around, settling between his legs with my back resting on his chest, and waited for his answer.

He kissed the top of my head and whispered, "I do. We were parked out on Old US 421. And I believe it was the same night you had that wardrobe malfunction."

I elbowed him in the ribs, "Hush. You ran off and left me there, alone!"

He wrapped his arms around my middle, and we began reminiscing.

We were backed up in the shipping area of an old warehouse, curled up in each other's arms, sweaty and warm. Alex was my first, and I was very naive and unskilled, but he was patient, and I was quite certain he enjoyed 'teaching me'. We had only been physical a few times prior, and I noticed tonight was different. It was as though he was more focused on me, his touches, his kisses, the passion in his eyes. It was that night he told me for the first time that he loved me. The night was perfect, until ...

We walked in the back door and found my parents sitting at the kitchen table playing cards. My dad and mom looked at us and then shot a look at one another and smirked.

Daddy looked up at Alex, "Was it any good?" Continuing to play the card game.

Alex and I looked quizzically at each other.

"Huh?" I asked. Puzzled at what he was asking.

"Son, was it any good?" Dad repeated.

This time we understood the question was geared toward Alex, but we were still baffled.

Dad then looked at me, called me by my nickname, and asked me if the sex was good. Mortified by my father's insinuation, I gaffed at him and denied everything, swearing we hadn't ... that I never. I swore to God and everything. But mom and dad sat staring at us, laughing, and that's when he said, "Look down at your clothes."

I looked down and, to my horror, found the tag of my romper flapping between my itty-bitty titties. Not only were my clothes on backward but inside out too!

I turned to look to Alex for ... hell, I don't know, an excuse. But that asshole had already cut a trail and was halfway out the door, leaving me to fend for myself.

"Bahahaha, the look on your face." Alex giggled.

I swat at him, "Asshole. You left me there alone ... in disgrace, after telling me, you love me. Ha!"

Alex reached for me and pulled me in against his chest, kissing the top of my head, "Never. I would never leave you, babygirl."

Bath Time Limbo

I don't remember when or why it began, but Alex and I started taking baths together. I would get in first, wash up, and then he would join me. I sometimes washed his body, and before I knew it, it became an every night thing, which I didn't mind. I enjoyed showing my love for him through this small act. And many, many times, the washing would lead to getting frisky.

One night, not long ago, we were in the tub for our usual nightly bath. The house was quiet, and I was feeling naughty.

I had just finished washing him and rinsing him off when I got this huge urge to take him in my mouth. Hell, who am I kidding? I was addicted to his dick. Anytime I was close to him, like laying my head in his lap. It was as though he was steel, and I was the magnet. I couldn't stop myself. I had to suck him off, and so that was how it began.

"No, stop. I was going to lose it if you don't stop, and I still want to turn you around and fuck the hell out of you. Of course, this wouldn't have been an issue back in the day, but that was seventy pounds ago, and I was much more limber and flexible.

"On your knees," he ordered.

I complied, and his hands reached up between my thighs, his thumb against my clit while his finger worked my inner walls. It drove me crazy, and I exploded.

"Stand up and put your foot here." He ordered, and I did as I was told.

His hand reached around, grasping my ass cheek, and pulled me flush against his face. But the angle wasn't right, and he was unable to get what he wanted. With a pull here and a push there, he had me all contorted up, and before I know it, I have a severe cramp. My foot slipped, and I went headfirst over the side of the tub. I tensed, convinced I was about to do a face plant to the floor, and it was going to hurt like a motherfucker, not to mention the embarrassment if I got seriously hurt. Our episode of The Day Sex sent me to the ER.

Suddenly Alex had a hold of me and somehow stopped my forward momentum, saving me from extreme pain and embarrassment.

We accept we are too old and fat to try that position again and retire it before laughing and getting out of the tub, drying off, and going to bed.

Splish 'n Splash Birthday

When you get to my age, birthdays are just another day, but not with Alex. He always makes sure my birthdays are special.

"Happy Birthday, babygirl."

I awake with him leaning over me, kissing my head, holding red roses in one hand and my favorite latte in the other.

"Rise and shine. You have a big day ahead of you." He promises.

Oh lord, what does he have up his sleeve? I know better than to ask, so I obey and crawl out of bed, taking my latte, sipping it before my feet hit the floor. Last night was crazy. I was still exhausted. Who knew two old goats could still fuck like that? My hoo-ha still aches, my ass was tender from the spankings, and my joints ache. I needed to look into that over-the-counter shit that swore it helped joints.

I take my roses and kiss him, "Thank you, Daddy." Carrying them to the kitchen, I found my trusty vase and put the flowers in some water.

"I was going to go run you a hot bath when you get finished here."

I step around the corner of the bedroom and into the bathroom. Candles are lit, and the tub is filled with scented bubbles. Daddy sat naked on the side of the tub, reaching his hand out for mine.

At the same time, a smile covers my face, and my pussy cried out in protest. I step closer and take his hand, lifting my foot and stepping into the steaming hot water. Slowly lowering myself, ahh, this feels so good. The water covers my body, leaving only my knees to stick out above the bubbles.

"I was going to give you a bath for a change."

"Oh, yes, sir."

He lathered the sponge and began washing every inch of my body. I could get used to this; no wonder he enjoyed his baths. Of course, I should have known he had ulterior motives, the horn dog.

As he attempted to lift me out of the water, he'd apparently forgotten my ass isn't as light as it once was, and the bubbles that clung to my skin would make me slippery. He lost his grip, and I slipped and fell back into the tub. Water and bubbles flying everywhere, soaking the curtains and the floor surrounding the tub.

"Ouch!" I cried out as my head hit the tub, and Alex's foot slipped in the water, sending him on top of me.

"Umph."

Alex tried to push himself off me, but his feet kept slipping in the water, and before we know it, we are both laughing hysterically. So much for being romantic.

It took way longer than it should for us to get out of the tub and dried off, but finally, we succeeded, and we're off to my first surprise.

Horseback riding.

Our own Route 69

The day had been wonderful. First, we went horseback riding and walked along the different trails. My hubs spoils me rotten in so many ways, but in turn, I spoil him too.

The sun was warm dappled light between the leaves of the trees, the muscles in my legs were beginning to cry out, and I needed a rest. We continued through the clearing until we came upon a gathering of trees along a rocky overlook. The boulders were perfect to rest on and hidden in the shade of the trees.

We slipped behind the biggest boulder and took a seat on two smaller ones; it was quiet. The birds singing and the breeze blowing through the leaves were the only sounds dancing above our heads. And the mood strikes!

"I wanna suck you," I state, looking sheepishly at Alex.

He immediately jumped to his feet and began unfastening his shorts.

Just the words off my lips have him semi and anxious. I love having the power and control over him and drop to my knees.

I worked him feverishly, my tongue, my teeth, my hands. He was weak-kneed and buzzing with excitement. I knew it wouldn't be long when he grabbed both sides of my head and began thrusting hard and fast. My gag reflex kicks in, and I try everything to keep from throwing up all over him. I was grasping his legs, and he's grasping my head; my eyes are watering, and as much as I hate to, I was going to have to tap out. But before I can, he stops immediately, turning away from me and hiding beside the giant rock. That was when I heard them ... Voices.

They are faint at first but grow louder and louder the closer they came. Just then, I saw something bright red, and a dark curly-haired little boy hopped around the boulder.

"Hi!" he said cheerfully, followed by his parents, "I have to go potty, and mommy says this is a good place to hide. Are you going potty too?" He walked over to Alex as he finishes fastening his pants, looking up at him.

"Umm, yep little champ. That's what I was doing."

"I don't see your spot." The little guy looked around, "Where did you pee?"

"Jeffrey! That is enough. Leave the man and lady alone." His mom chastised him.

I quickly stand, and Alex and I hurry back around the rocks and onto the trail.

"That was close!" I giggled.

Alex said nothing, a growl the only sound that comes from his throat. Then, grabbing my hand, he pulled me forward. I had trouble keeping up with him.

"What's your hurry?"

He stayed silent and continued pulling me down the path and up the hill to the parking area and our car.

"Get in."

Perplexed by his behavior, I stand and look at him.

He opened his door and got in, looking over at me, "Well? Come on, get your ass in the car."

I sat down, closing my door before asking him, "What's going on? What the hell was all that about?"

He said nothing, just started the car and backed out of the parking spot. His hand dropped to his zipper and began to unzip his pants, freeing himself.

"Remember those days you'd suck my cock while I drove down the interstate?"

I couldn't say a word, just pasted a cheesy smile on my face as my stomach quivered like jello. The memories flooded my mind, and once again, I was grateful he had driven the truck today. It had a bench seat with a console that folded down, or you could flip it up to make 'room'. And I didn't waste any time. In one swift movement, my purse was tossed on the floor, the console flipped up, and I was doing a nosedive beneath the steering wheel. Everything was going great at first. I was feeling proud I hadn't lost my touch after all these years, until ...

"Shit! Hold still. A semi is getting ready to pass."

No problem, it wasn't the first time I'd gotten caught doing this going seventy mph down the interstate. I'd just tilt my head and pretend I was sleeping with my head in his lap like I used to.

Wrong!

Don't ask me how it happened because I have no fucking clue. It has never happened before. But somehow, my head got trapped between the steering wheel and his lap, well, cock. Might as well call a spade a spade, right? I twisted this way and that a couple of times and even caused the truck to swerve.

"Hold still. You're going to get us killed." Alex barked.

"I can't move! I'm stuck!"

By now, the semi-truck is running alongside us, fender to fender. The co-driver apparently looked over and down into our truck. Because the next thing I know, he was blowing his air horn and cheering us on. I thought I could never be more mortified ...

That was until we stopped at the exit 53 Truck Stop. We went in to use the restroom and get a drink. As we walked out, a big truck pulled up next to our truck and stopped. It got our attention. We looked up, and it was the same damn truck. The driver rolled down his window and shouted, "I bet she could suck a watermelon through a garden hose!"

Red Lobster

We drove for another two hours before pulling off the interstate. My stomach was growling, and my head was beginning to pound.

We kept passing restaurant after restaurant until finally turning into a Red Lobster. Yes! Finally.

The wait wasn't too bad, maybe ten or fifteen minutes, and then we were seated. As always, Alex ordered the stuffed mushrooms, and we pigged out on the garlic cheese biscuits and mushrooms. I waited until Alex ordered before I decided I was going all out and ordered lobster.

We enjoyed each other's company. I had a couple of margaritas, and by the time our meal was delivered to our table, I was feeling a little tipsy.

Alex had ordered the ultimate seafood, him and his crab legs. When they came, the waitress apologized that they didn't have any clean pliers, and without missing a beat, my adorable husband reached into his pants pocket and said, "Don't worry about it, I've got a pair." Pulling out a mini pair of dirty pliers he used at work and began cracking the shells. Don't get me wrong, I love crab too, but I wasn't working that hard for my meal. So, lobster it was, and it was delicious. So, what if the sweet, melted butter dripped from my chin occasionally. I was in my element.

Finishing off my last bite, I wiped my mouth and rested my hand on my full stomach, "Oh my gawd, that was so good! I wasn't expecting Red Lobster."

Alex looked across the table at me and said, "You should feel privileged; the last woman I fucked got a cheeseburger."

Role Play

6 8 9 – 5 4 3 6 ... ring.

"Hey, you sexy thang."

His voice sang through my ear, bringing an instant smile to my face.

"Hey, yes. This is Lisa Gail. I um need someone to come and look at my washing machine. It's leaking water."

Clearing his throat, "Huhumm, well, yes, ma'am. I think we can get you taken care of. I don't have any openings today. But I can get you in tomorrow."

"Oh no. I don't have any clean underwear, and I need to do laundry today."

"Well, I reckon I can come by this evening, but it'll cost you time and a half. And I ain't cheap."

Relief washes over me, "Yes, that's fine. I don't care how much it costs. I'm sure we can work something out; I'm willing to do ... *anything.*" I add a sweet twist to my voice.

"Well. I'll see you around six this evening, and Miss Lisa ..."

"Yes, sir."

"I look forward to seeing you..." His voice trailed off, leaving his statement open.

5:30 rolled around, and my stomach was getting anxious. I decided to spice it up a little, peeling off one layer of clothing at a time. I slipped into my robe. This would be good.

There was a knock on the door as I finished putting on a thick layer of bright red lipstick. Pressing my lips together, smearing the lipstick along both lips before be-bopping to the door.

I stopped at the door, "Who is it?"

"Your handyman, here to look at your washer."

I opened the door and welcomed him in, "Thank you so much for coming after hours. I cannot express to you how grateful I am."

His eyes zeroed in on my rosy, red lips, "Not a problem." He shifted the weight of the toolbox in his hand.

I turned and led him to the laundry room.

"Well, let's see what's going on here." He opened his toolbox and brought out a screwdriver.

My eyes widened in surprise, "Oh my, you have such *big* tools." I said seductively, swiping my tongue over my bottom lip before biting it.

He leaned over the washer and began to unscrew the cover.

I checked my cleavage and made sure my itty bitties were on full display before I leaned over next to him and gave him a full-frontal view. "Is there anything I can do to help?"

He looked up from his work and slowly perused my chest up to my lips. "Ma'am, do you have any idea of the distraction you are causing?"

He squirmed and pushed his pelvis against the washer as though to stifle an erection. The feral look in his eyes ramped up, and the butterflies in my stomach and my hoo-ha clenched in anticipation. His eyes finally made it up to my face, and he opened his mouth to speak. His sexy raspy voice melted my panties, "Are you teasing me?"

Twirling my hair with my finger, I dropped it down and traced it along my cleavage, "Who? Me!"

I bit my lip as I watched his cobalt eyes change to a sexy, dusty gray, and my insides quivered with excitement.

Before I knew it, he'd lifted me onto the dryer, his hands all over me. My breath came in heavy pants as he ripped my shirt off me.

A mere moment passes, and we are both panting, and the dryer rocks back and forth, bouncing against the wall. We were both lost in the moment as he continued to plow into me over and over, oblivious we were fucking in front of the window or that our neighbor was right outside our door.

Rainy With a Chance Of

It was a gloomy rainy day, and the two of us were curled up in the bed watching the local news after dinner, waiting for our favorite sitcom M*A*S*H.

The weatherman finished with his forecast, and I roll over to my hubs, snuggling up next to him.

"Look, Friday's temp is your favorite number, and so is Sunday. Who knows, maybe you'll get lucky," I giggled and shrugged, "There's a sixty-nine percent chance."

He grabbed hold of me and began tickling me before smothering my mouth with his. "I'll show you sixty-nine percent." He breathed in my ear, drawing me down the pillow and beneath his body.

I can't help myself, and I started giggling. Before I knew it, I had a complete giggle fest.

"Seriously?" He rolled off me, threw his arm over his head, and palmed the remote in his hand. Huffing, he began changing the tv channels. His bottom lip swelled, and he began to pout.

I leaned up on my elbow and hovered over the top of him, "For a grown-ass man, you are so adorable when you pout." Leaning down, I kissed his forehead, "I'm sorry." I giggled again.

Pushing me away, his bottom lip bulged out, and in a whiny kid voice, "No, you aren't ... you laughed at me. I was trying to get my mojo on, and you laughed!"

Roll with the Punches

We had gone on another road trip. It was early fall, and the leaves had begun changing. Alex surprised me with a trip to the mountains. He knew fall was my favorite time of year, the smells, colors, and the crisp air. It was perfect in every way. We had been driving for hours, up up up further and further until we were driving alongside the clouds. The road wound around the mountain and dipped along the hills. It was a wonderful day; the weather was perfect as the sun peaked through the clouds as they drifted across the sky.

We stopped at one of the scenic lookouts and got out of the car. We held hands and walked along the pathway, listening to the many voices that echoed through the trails' trees. We laughed and kissed and took pictures. It was a wonderful time.

"Want to go even higher?" Alex asked.

"Yes!" I quickly responded, and he led our way back to the car.

I had never been to this area of our state, so I didn't know much about it. Alex being the history buff, shared information he knew about the area and the many tales told about it and the settlers.

It was the first sunny weekend we had had in a little over a month, and everyone was suffering from cabin fever. The narrow winding roads were busy. It wasn't uncommon to drive a few yards and have to slow to almost a stop and ease your car off onto the shoulder to let another vehicle pass coming from the other direction. We had been doing this for about two hours when we finally came upon another lookout.

This one was smaller, and it had a couple of placards with information about the native birds and animals in the area. Also, a warning against leaving food out and the bears that inhabited the area.

Alex and I were still at the overlook admiring the view for a few moments before he dropped his hand from my side and began walking around the overlook and down the side of the mountain.

"Where are you going?" I asked.

"I got to pee." He replied, disappearing behind a tree.

I waited, looking around, watching for other people. But we were the only ones in the area. So, when Alex's head popped around the tree, and he began back up the path, I asked him. "Is there any room for me to squat?"

"Sure, just be careful."

At this point, my bladder was screaming. I knew it was now or never. And it wasn't like I had never peed in the great outdoors. Hell, I used to have to do it all the time when I was a kid. Mom and dad would drag me fishing, and there I would be, bored as hell and needing to pee. My momma taught me how to pull my short leg to the side and pee without pulling my pants down.

So, I was quite confident that I could handle this little feat.

The path was still muddy from the previous day's rain, and some places were slippery. I followed Alex's instructions and kept to the left of the path so as not to fall. Turning, I looked back to see if the coast was still clear and made my way over to the tree.

The ground was in a slope, of course, it was; it was on the side of a fucking mountain. But there were rocks settled in the earth, making it look like steps. I put one foot on one rock and the other foot on the other rock and wished like hell I was wearing a pair of shorts, but as I said, it was fall, and it was a tad bit nippy. So, I unbuttoned and unzipped my jeans and pulled them down to my ankles.

Carefully, I bent my knees and squatted. Ha, I still got it. I balanced on the balls of my feet while I let go. Suddenly I remember how much I hated 'drip drying', as they call it. I looked down and noticed the pee was beginning to puddle and run down the embankment toward my foot and the bottom of my jeans. Oh, no, no, no!

I cut it off mid-stream. My thigh muscles began to cramp, and I needed to stand before they gave way. My head began to swim a little, and I started to wobble. Trying to right my balance, I leaned forward a little as I tried to stand, but it was too late. I lost my balance and fell back. Landing in a pool of Alex and my piss and some greenery, I prayed wasn't poison ivy. I felt my body start to lean to the left, and fear encased me. I could see myself now, bare ass rolling down the side of this mountain. Not being as they once were, my reflexes sent me on a whole new level of falling on my ass. I involuntarily screamed, and Alex came rushing to the edge of the path.

"Are you ok?"

All he could see was my muddy, piss-soaked bare ass staring back at him.

"Yeah, I'm fucking peachy," I yelled back at him as I tried to untangle my feet and stop from falling to my death. Hoping I could cover my nakedness before the people in the car that just pulled up got out and saw me.

I finally righted myself and pulled my jeans up, and it wasn't until I come around the tree, I saw Alex grinning from ear to ear, trying his damnedest not to laugh.

I pointed my finger at him and dared him, "Don't you say a fucking word."

I managed to get myself back up the path and into the car by the time the other vehicle passengers were out and walking around.

Alex, on the other hand, is biting back his laughter as he gets in the car, starting it and backing up.

He glanced at me, and I growled.

"I hope to hell that wasn't poison ivy my fat ass landed in."

Alex turned the wheels, and we pulled out of the overlook and began winding around the curves once again. We make it approximately five hundred yards when I spot it.

A fucking bathroom!

In the Still of the Night

It was a warm spring night, and we decided to build a fire in the pit and enjoy the evening. The crickets were calling, and the frogs were singing, and in the distance, we could hear the mating calls of the coyote. It was perfect. The week had been a hellish one, Aunt Flo wreaked havoc on my insides, and there was the one day I thought my vagina was going to fall out. But all of that was over, and my girlie bits were zinging with anticipation.

The sky was ink black with white twinkling specks, and occasionally a satellite would skip across the sky. The only other light was that provided by the fire.

A dirty little thought crossed my mind, and I hesitated for a moment and then decided to go for it.

I stood and walked over in front of my husband. He looked up at me, questioning as he smoked his cigar and drank his bourbon and Coke.

I said nothing as my eyes pierced his, and I dropped to my knees. It was then he realized what I was going to do.

Reaching out, I unbuttoned his shorts and lowered his zipper, slipping my hand inside, freeing him from the confinement of his shorts.

My belly quickened with excitement, and my mouth watered. He was semi-erect, and I love the power I have over him. Feeling him grow hard and thick inside my mouth gave me a thrill I am unable to explain. I worked him into a frenzy and reached down between my legs and began swirling my finger around my bundle of nerves.

It was like he has a radar that tells him anytime I touch myself. I know this because his whole body shifts, the playing field has changed, and he's burning with fire.

Before I knew it, he stood, pulling me to my feet and toward the car. Jerking my pants down, he turned me facing the car and shoved my shoulders down against the hood, and kicked my feet apart in the process. His hot breath was against my ear, and he hissed, "I'm going to fuck you right here in front of God and everybody. Are you ready?"

Holy fuck, my knees turned to jelly, and I locked them in place, begging, "Yes, please."

He thrust forward, but his cock slipped and slid up my ass crack, "Oops."

He backed up and took aim; this time, it slipped between my thighs and missed the mark.

I was panting and dying inside. I wanted to feel him so badly, and the fact we are doing this outside in our yard where anyone can see only added to the excitement.

He flipped me around and tried to lift me onto the hood and spread my legs. We quickly realized the car is too far off the ground, and he'd need a step stool to reach because standing on his toes just won't get it done.

"Son of a bitch."

I inched myself down a little at a time, trying to reach, but I was unsuccessful. I can't wait any longer; I have to have him.

Not paying attention, I slid down off the hood. My foot landed on loose gravel and flew out from under me. My ass hit the grill, bumper, and finally the ground.

I cry out in pain, he screamed in fear, and the neighbors front porch light comes on.

Shit!!

With his shorts around his ankles and me without any bottoms, we scrambled on our hands and knees around the car and out of sight. My ass cheeks were on fire from the landing, and my knees and hands were scuffed. My ass was still in the air, and he saw it as a perfect opportunity. *Slam*! Right into me. Instant orgasm, I screamed in ecstasy, and the other neighbors turned on their porch light. We were surrounded, but my sweet husband kept on plowing until we both reached the pinnacle, we were desperate to reach.

Tequila Makes Your Clothes Fall Off

The waitress sat the two shot glasses of tequila down on our table, just the thought made me gag, and Alex snickered.

"Hey, it was not my fault," I reminded him. "Those nephews of mine set me up."

Alex rolled his eyes and shook his head, "Yeah, right. They held your nose and forced you to take those shots."

We were out to dinner with some friends when Alex decided to share a story about me that he will never let me live down.

We were at the bowling alley for my cousin's son's third birthday. The kids and adults were laughing and playing. My oldest nephew showed up, and we are all talking when he slipped away, announcing he was heading to the bar.

Bar!

My latest favorite drink of choice was tequila, and I was in the mood for a shot. I had just eaten lunch and knew it would be safe, 'cause I was a lightweight.

I found myself walking up beside Matt and asking him if he'd like to buy his favorite aunt a shot of tequila.

I should have known when I saw the glint in his eyes. I should have retracted my request and turned and walked away, but no. I was too damn stubborn.

"Well, hell yeah!" He reached over, putting his arm around my shoulders, and pulled me close. "Hey, give my aunt here a shot of tequila."

The barmaid looked up and nodded. She asked which one and began naming different brands. I had no idea. I was a newbie with a small pocketbook. I drank the cheap shit.

"Only the best for my favorite aunt."

The barmaid sat a tall shot glass, and when I say a tall glass, I mean a glass that holds two fucking shots, not the usual one I was used to. I sprinkled some salt on my hand, licked, took a swig, and bit my lime.

"Wow, this shit is smooth." The clear liquid tingled my throat as it trickled down into my stomach, and the warmth slowly radiated through my body. Heck yeah. I looked at the glass. "Wait a minute; I just took a swig. Who put more tequila in my glass?"

Laughing, Matt informed me, "Hey, that's a real shot glass. It ain't one of those pussy glasses you are used to. This is a real shot glass. Drink up."

By now, one of my other nephews, the Mr. Goodie Two Shoes, had to stick his nosey ass in.

"Yeah, come on, Aunt *Lisa*," I hated the way he said my name. "Drink it all, or you're a pussy."

"Fuck you, you little prick."

And down goes the rest, smooth and silky. I slammed the glass down on the bar and flipped him off before swinging my legs around and standing up walking away from the bar. I made my way back to the bowling lanes we were stationed at and took my seat. I was minding my own business and wasn't bothering anyone. So, what if I had asked my niece if she wanted to see a naked picture of Alex. I was only joking. Duh.

The next thing I knew, Alex was standing beside me, telling me to get my purse and jacket, and he was taking me home.

"What! Why?" I asked.

All eyes are on me. What's everyone looking at? I wondered to myself.

Alex leaned in beside my ear and whispered, "You're drunk."

"What? No, I am not. I just had a shot, and it was on a full stomach, sooo there." At the time, I didn't realize I was slurring. "I'm ffffine."

"No, sweetheart, it's time to go. I'll get you home and into bed."

"Really?" I squealed, "Are you going to fuck me too?"

I tried to stand, and I swore someone jerked my stool out from under me.

"Shhhhh!" Alex placed his hand over my mouth as I fall off the stool, "Come on, baby girl."

By the time we made it home, I realize Alex knew what the hell he was talking about. My ass was *drunk*. He helped me in the house and tried to put me to bed, but I was insistent on having drunk sex. I've always heard you should at least have drunk sex once in your life, and I was not getting any younger.

To be honest, I can't remember much about the sex. However, I do know Alex conceded because my husband never turns down sex.

When I woke up, the house is quiet, and I felt like I was alone in bed. I rolled over to check, and boy, what a mistake that was. The whole room flipped and began to spin. I knew right away this wasn't good. I could feel my stomach lurch, and I tried to stand up. I've got to get to the bathroom. My feet kept getting tangled, and the room wouldn't stop spinning. I held on to the door frame, the furniture, the shower stall, and the wall making it across the lavatory's threshold and falling to my knees just as my chin hit the seat of the toilet and the ride began.

My stomach began convulsing, and my head split in blinding pain. My throat was on fire as the volcanic lava spewed forth. My body heaved, and my head shivered as the alcohol and bile bubbled up, erupting from my body. I swear I needed an exorcism. My body had been taken over by an evil demon. Or while I slept, aliens landed and snatched my body. Either way, I was certain I was going to die. Hell, I wanted to die. Death had to be better than this.

I prayed, '*God, help me*' in between fits of vomit and '*Please, let me die*'.

The room kept spinning faster and faster and faster it went. *I swear I will never drink again!* I promised.

Alex must have heard me because he brought me a cool, wet washcloth and placed it on the back of my neck before tossing me my pillow and a blanket on the floor beside me. And I was quite certain he laughed as he turned and walked away, leaving me to burn in the pits of hell alone.

Country Music Hall of Fame

It was the end of the spring semester for our youngest. She was the only one of our three kids who decided to go to college, and her daddy and I were so proud of her. We had made arrangements to drive down to Bowling Green to pick her and all her belongings up. Alex got the idea of going down a few days early, getting a hotel room in Nashville and seeing the sights, and enjoying some 'us' time before we lost our freedom again.

It was a beautiful evening, and the sunset was breathtaking as we drove down the interstate. Finally, we arrived and found a hotel. It was late, and we both had been up early that morning and worked a full day. We showered, crashed, and burned. I didn't even wake up to go pee during the night.

When I awoke the next morning, Alex was coming out of the bathroom, "Hey, sleepyhead. You want this coffee or a good cup?" Pointing at the mini coffee maker beside the sink.

Stretching, "That's a no-brainer."

Leaning over, he kissed my head and swatted my backside. "Be right back." And out the door, he went.

I used this time to get dressed, put my face on and fix my unruly hair. I was finishing up last-minute touch-ups as Alex walked through the door, breakfast in hand and a caramel frappe. Yum!!

Reaching for it, "You know the way to my heart." I took a long drag off the straw. The sweet caramel freeze dissolved in my mouth, and I swallowed, "Mmmm, this is so good!" We ate our breakfast, packed up, and walked out into a wet, dreary day.

We got back on the interstate drive around Nashville and got off another exit that took us to the downtown area. Alex parked the car, and we got out. The rain had stopped mostly. For now, there was just a soft mist in the air.

Alex took my hand and led me down Broadway.

Before I knew it, we walked along the very same sidewalks country legends had walked before us. Hank Williams Sr AND Jr., Roy Clark, Elvis Presley, Barbara Mandrell, Laura Alaina, my idol, Martina McBride, and many more. It was amazing to see some of the 'hole in the wall' honky-tonks where some of the most famous country singers began. We turned a corner, and right before our eyes was the Ryman Auditorium and The Country Music Hall of Fame.

It was surreal.

We climbed the steps of the CMHoF and entered. The lights glistened off the glass cases filled with memorabilia.

Elvis's pink Cadillac, a lifelike bust of him along with some of his infamous sequined outfits and scarves. Rows and rows of famous musicians and the history behind them. We turned the corner, and there in the center, Garth Brooks and Tricia Yearwood.

The excitement continued to build inside me as the music played through the speakers, and before I knew it, my whole body was zinging. And the naughty bitch inside me erupted.

Across the hall from where we stood was a family restroom. My girlie parts were tingling, and I wanted to scratch that itch if you know what I mean.

"Psst," I called to Alex to get his attention as he was reading about Garth Brooks and motioned with my head towards the bathroom. It didn't take him a nanosecond to guess what I was inferring to.

We rushed into the bathroom and locked the door. I raised up to kiss him and asked in my best husky, seductive voice, "Ever fucked in the Country Music Hall of Fame?"

His eyes turned smoldering, and his hands were all over me. He marched me back against the sink, and for a split second, my brain kicked in, 'what if the sink doesn't hold and we break it?' I looked down and spotted a step stool, bingo! It was fate. It was meant to be the sex gods wanted us the fuck in the Hall of Fame. In front of a huge mirror, *score*!

I dropped my shorts and let them fall to my ankles and bent over, resting my hands on the stool as Alex unzipped his jeans and took aim.

Bam! I see stars as he plunged inside me. The excitement, the thrill, the naughtiness was euphoric.

The stool began to walk across the floor with each of our thrusts but paying it no mind, we continue, and the stool started to thump against the floor in rhythm. Thump ... Thump. Thump. Thump! Faster and faster, we have lift off!

We both reached our intended goal and took a picture to commemorate the outlandish event.

I mean, who else can say they fucked in the Country Music Hall of Fame?

Engine #3

I have to say, one of my favorite unique places Alex and I got it on was good ol' engine #3. Not many people can say they fucked on a fire truck, but we can, and we did *twice*!

It was time for the engine to have some touch-up cosmetic work, the red paint was fading, and the stickers were peeling. So, the fire chief brought her up to Alex's work. Alex has magical hands. I swear I don't think there is anything that man can't do.

It was a Saturday, and Alex had decided to go into the shop for a few hours to put some brakes on my car and change the oil. He and I love role-playing, and that day he was my personal mechanic.

We pulled inside the garage, and the first thing I noticed is a big white fire engine with red block lettering sitting in the last bay. My girlie parts were zinging, and I looked over to Alex; he knows me so well. Without saying a word, he took my hand and led me over to it. Immediately entering his role as a tour guide.

"Good afternoon. Have you ever been this close to a fire engine?" he asked.

I acted shy and batted my eyes a little before biting my lip and looking away.

He reached his hand out and turned my face toward his, "Don't be bashful, or is it the size that scares you?"

I bit my lip again and feign a sweet southern accent, "Well, I have never seen one this big before. It is quite ... intimidating. Can I ... touch it?"

He smiled and took my hand, "Oh, sweetheart, you can touch anything you want." Stepping up onto the truck, he held out his hand for me to take.

"Here, let me help you."

He pulled me up onto the platform, opened the third door behind the driver's seat, and invited me to enter.

"Come on in, don't be afraid, touch it." He insisted.

So, I did. My hands trembled in anticipation as I reached out and ran my hand along the cool leather seats. My breath hitched, and a sigh escaped my lips.

"You like?" he asked.

"Oh, yes. I love it, and the smell ..." I inhaled deeply through my nose to drive the point. "It's ... it's ..."

"It's calling you." He finished my thought, "Here, take a seat, feel the leather beneath your thighs. The power and authority that radiates within this cab are intoxicating. Isn't it?"

Sitting in the huge seat, the leather is cool against the skin of my legs, but the inside of my thighs is ablaze. *What's happening to me?*

I was unable to reply to his last question. It was as though I was spellbound, and he was a wizard. My thoughts and my body are no longer my own. He controlled me, my breathing, my heart beats, my desire. And at that moment, I desired to feel my naked ass against those leather seats.

It was as though he read my mind because he took my hand and helped me to stand. Then, I slowly unfastened the button and lowered the zipper, letting my bottoms fall to the fire truck floor.

He gently pushed me back and lowered me to the seat.

"Ohhh." The leather was cold against my fevered ass, and I loved it.

He pulled my knees apart and settled himself between my feet. With his eyes blazing with passion, he slowly brought his face to the apex of my thighs. Stopping for a moment, he looked up and smiled, "I've never eaten pussy in a fire truck before," dipping his head, he moves in for the kill.

It was instant electricity; my back arched, and the flames ignited. The coolness from the seat, the heat from his mouth, and the vibration beneath me ... Wait!

What? What the hell is vibrating? I jumped, and my arm hit the control panel. The lights come on, and the area surrounding us is coated in cascading red lights.

Shit! What did I just do?

Alex placed one hand on my stomach, pushing me back down in the seat, and the other hand flipped off the light switch. With one swipe of his tongue, he had me forgetting everything. He worked my body feverishly before standing me up and bending me over. We began to go at it slowly at first, but the fire built, and soon we were in the center of an inferno. Finally, neither of us could stand it anymore, and we let loose. The truck rocked back and forth, and sweat poured off us, making us slippery. Suddenly my foot slipped, and we tumble forward, the horn blew, and the lights came back on, and through it all, Alex never broke stride. Damn, what a man!

Any given day, while driving through town, it wasn't unusual for us to pass engine #3, and when we do, we simply look at one another and smile.

Bourbon on the Rocks

Alex took me for a drive after dinner one night, and we ended up going to a small community on the outskirts of our town. It was one of our many make-out areas from our past, out on an old, crooked country road. The farther we drove, the cooler the air became. The road was lined with horse farms, streams, hills, native flowers and led to one of Kentucky's finest bourbon distilleries.

As we drove through the countryside, the sweet scent of honeysuckle, horse manure, and bourbon mash lingered in the air, pulling us back in time. It seemed like yesterday, not thirty-four years. And here we were, back in this very same spot.

The sun had set, and darkness had shrouded us. The gentle cascade of the water trickling over the dam where we sat parked in the truck was the only sound.

"Remember when ..." Alex began.

Before he finished what he was saying, I had hopped over the seat and was pawing at his shirt, desperate to get it off him.

He opened his door and quickly shimmied out of his shorts. It didn't take me long to follow suit. And then I leaned back against my door and smiled, motioning, 'come here,' with my finger.

He lifted one foot up and onto the truck and lifted himself off the wet rock we were parked on.

"Hold it right there!" A deep voice echoed around us. "This place is off-limits; you're trespassing."

"Shit!" We both hissed.

I grabbed my tank top and quickly threw it over my head and put my arms through the armholes as Alex jumped in the truck, slamming his door and throwing the truck in reverse.

The tires spun on the moss-covered dam before finally catching, jetting us back and away from the voice and the guard it belonged to.

Alex cut the wheels and threw the truck into drive as the wheels squealed against the asphalt, throwing rocks in our wake.

"Son of a bitch." Alex huffed, slamming his hand on the steering wheel.

I was frozen in my seat. My sweaty bare ass was sticking to the leather seat as he took the curves out and away from the distillery. I looked over at him and began laughing. It was a giggle at first, but then ... my stomach began hurting from the deep and heavy laughs barreling up and out of my throat.

Alex slowed and stopped the truck, "What the hell is so funny?"

I can't speak because of the laughter, so I point at him.

He looked down at his naked form, his manhood no longer at attention but instead had hung its head in shame.

He too began to laugh, "I'm beginning to see a pattern here."

I swallowed down the remaining giggles and replied, "We've got to stop meeting like this."

He shook his head and looked in the rearview mirror. With no cars in sight, he opened his door and slipped out, stepping back into his shorts. Closing his door, he looked over and said, "To be continued."

All Choked Up

"Hey, Beck," I hug and kiss her. "I've missed so much!"

She hugs and kisses my cheek. "I've missed you! So?"

The hostess leads us to a patio table, "Your server will be right out."

We both smile and take our seats.

"I hope it's the same dude we had last time we were here. I had so much fun with him."

Beckee looks across the table at me and gives me the stink eye while drumming her fingers on the table impatiently.

"What?" I ask.

"I'm waiting for all the juicy deets. Do not spare any. I want everything laid on the table."

I look at her questioningly.

"Details, Lisa, details. I want all the damn details."

"Details? Of what?" I love playing dumb, and I was good at it.

Just then, our server appears. Sadly, it's not the same young man, but a different one. This one seems possibly a bit older. He takes our drink order and walks away.

Slap!

"Ouch, son of a bitch. What the hell was that for?" I demand as I rub my arm. "You skanky ass bitch, that hurt."

The server appears at our table and watches us for a moment before setting our drinks down.

"Do you ladies need more time?"

And like a flip of a switch, we are both smiling as if nothing happened as we look up at him.

"I'm ready. I'll have the pecan chicken salad with ranch, please."

Beckee thinks for a moment, "Oh, that does sound good. I'll have one too."

The server writes down our order and turns just as Beckee throws an ice cube at me and calls me a slut bucket.

He pauses for a second and walks off, shaking his head.

"I love you so much." I declare as Beckee rolls her eyes.

"Damn it, Lisa Gail, am I going to have to drag it out of you?"

I must admit I enjoyed watching her squirm a bit more than I should, but it's been way too long since she and I had quality time together, and I've missed aggravating her.

I take a sip of my tea and stretch my arms out in front of me, popping my knuckles and peering around as though I was about to really reveal some top security secret shit

"You were right," I mumbled to her.

Her eyes grow huge, "Wait, what did you just say? I don't think I heard you."

Bitch.

So, I raised my voice a little and repeated myself, "I said you were right."

"Hahahaha. I cannot believe it. Lisa Gail Collins needed me to help her in the sex department. Holy hell, everyone get under your table; the world is coming to an end." She yells.

This time I whacked her on the arm, "You skank."

"Bitch."

"Slut."

"Whore."

I gasp at her, "No, I'm not. I've never charged, and you know it!"

And we both burst out in a fit of laughter.

"Ok, so I started reading the book, Fifty Shades and as you said, it was magical. It was damn near an aphrodisiac, a Viagra in book form. It had both of us clawing and panting all over the other.

Alex, oh my fucking gawd, Beck, I thought he was virile when we were young but damn! He damn well nearly killed me a few times. You know, when we were young, neither of us really knew what we were doing. Hell, back then, he called himself short stroke. But now, his mind, his body, his aura is mature, he's in control, and he lasts forever. There were a few times I was thinking, hurry up, damn it, blow already, ya know?

But he'd keep right on going.

I felt I needed to tap out a few times. But you know me, I was too damn stubborn for that. So, what if I walked like I had been riding all day bareback … I reckon you could say I was." Laughing at my own joke.

Beckee sat and listened, she laughed, and there were times I thought perhaps she didn't believe some of the events until I showed her the pics.

"Oh my god, Lisa! Your twat is posing!" she laughed.

And when I showed her the photo from the Country Music Hall of Fame, her eyes damn near fell out. There we were standing in front of the mirror, Alex taking the pic of us; I was bent over with him flush against my bare ass.

I began telling her about our first BDSM session. She spits tea across the table all over me, laughing her ass off. I just sat there wiping my arms and face off, waiting for her convulsions to stop.

"I don't know what's so damn funny about the word banana!" I snip at her. Only to have her start laughing again, this time she starts snorting like a pig and clamps her legs together,

"Ohhh, my God!" she gasps, "I'm going to piss myself!" Beckee laughs and snorts again, "Banana … for a safe word!"

Bahaha bitch.

"Oh, for fucks sake, what would you have chosen for your safe word, smart ass?" I ask.

She gasps again and attempts to calm herself with slow deep breaths.

"I don't know ... maybe asparagus!" she starts laughing hysterically.

"I hate you."

Laughing, she reaches for my hand, "I know."

I jerk my hand away and cross my arms in a huff, "You're never going to let me live this down, are you?"

She shakes her head side to side.

"You ready for book two?"

A Special Note

I was asked to write the last chapter in my wife's latest book, so here it goes.

First and foremost, I hope you have enjoyed reading about Lisa and Alex's escapades.

But did you know most of these stories are true? These stories were set into place some 33 years ago when I was attracted by one helluva set of sexy eyes that, to this very day, still push my buttons. And when I look into them, I still get lost.

KC is a remarkable woman who has raised three kids and put up with one horny ass husband. And now, she is chasing her dreams by writing books. By the way, she says I get horny anytime the wind blows. And yep, she's right. I am so proud of her and what she has accomplished so far, and I will forever love and support her.

After 33 years, people ask, "How do you keep the fire burning?" The answer is simple. I'm KC's research partner, and I can't go wrong there. But on a serious note, although we've gotten older and gravity has taken over, things don't quite work like they once did. We have simply adjusted and improvised to maintain our way of life. It also helps when your soulmate is someone easy to love and live with. I will always put her first and will continue to as long as there is breath left in my body. What Babygirl wants, Babygirl gets.

Thank you again for spending your hard-earned money on KC's books. I hope life finds you happy and humble.

Yours,

Carl AKA Aldie AKA Daddy

Don't miss out!

Visit the website below and you can sign up to receive emails whenever K.C. Rice publishes a new book. There's no charge and no obligation.

https://books2read.com/r/B-A-ZITB-QRMPB

BOOKS 2 READ

Connecting independent readers to independent writers.

About the Author

Considers herself just a simple country girl, born and raised in Frankfort, Kentucky.

Her first love will always be painting. Sitting in front of a blank canvas allowing the brush strokes and oils to illustrate her story.

In 2014 she tried her hand at creative writing and realized she had discovered a new passion.

She is now a Best Selling Multi-genre Author, and you can find her books on most ebook outlets. If you'd like a signed copy of her printed books, please email her at authorkcrice@gmail.com

Read more at www.pureromancekcrice.com.